Carolina Key

a Mountain Creek Mystery

vol. 1

Elizabeth Truiett

Carolina Key

Dedicated to:

Boyd Edwards

The best husband in the world.

You told me I could do it!

I love you.

Sun. July 8, 2008
Hope

When I learned Shirley Baker was dead I knew I must disappear. For good. There was only one place in which to make this happen. It was a little island called Carolina Key just west of Port Aransas. As I drove from my home in Mountain Creek, just outside of Austin, I tried not to panic. The heat of summer simmered on the pavement as mile after mile I alternately prayed to God for protection and tried to figure a way out. If only he didn't know what I had found...

Thurs. July 5, 2008
Hope

"Mom, where is the tomato sauce?" I turned from stacking loaves of bread in the storeroom to see my 15 year old daughter Grace, lean around the door.

"It should be in the can pantry," I replied.
"Ok, how many cans do we need?" she asked.

"Fourteen regular cans or five #10 cans," I said. We were in charge of preparing dinner for 120 campers, counselors, and staff at Indian Oaks, a Christian camp for inner city youth in the cedar lined hill country of Central Texas. We were located in the town of Mountain Creek. Grace, tall, thin and beautiful with golden brown hair and a sunburned nose was a junior counselor this year. I volunteered every year for the past three years to work in the kitchen cooking and washing dishes. This was basically what I did at home anyway, just on a smaller scale.

We retrieved the cans and went back to the kitchen to make the sauce. After frying the ground beef and tearing up 8 heads of lettuce we were ready to serve. The spaghetti dinner was a success. The children loved it and I watched with satisfaction at the looks on their faces as they slurped the tomato sauce covered noodles. The sound in the dining hall was deafening, with forks clattering to the floor and the kids giggling and screaming.

Shirley Baker, the owner of the camp, came over. She placed her clipboard on the counter and blew out a breath.

"Boy it's hot today. Hope, don't forget, we have that health inspector on Tuesday, so get the jcs (junior counselors) to do some extra scrubbing this weekend."

"No problem," I said.

Now it was our turn to eat. I loaded my plate with salad and took a small portion of the spaghetti. I was watching my weight, as always. Monday was my weigh in day. Little did I know that by Monday night I would be buried alive in the hot sand in Carolina Key fighting for everything I held dear but fearing the worst.

Ch. 2
Hope

Thursday night at Indian Oaks was the night the counselors reenacted the crucifixion of Jesus. The reenactment brought to life details and emotions these world weary teens knew little about. They knew much about survival but not about eternal life, salvation or hope in Jesus. Some of them had never seen a bible before. At Indian Oaks, a bible was issued to each camper right away, even before their cabin assignments. The reenactment occurred right after dinner.

Grace, who had been excused from dish duty, and was playing the part of Mary the mother of Jesus, was getting into her costume when a flurry of teenage girls entered my kitchen.

"Mama Stephens, Mama Stephens! You totally have to help us. Chelsea's dress is ripped because retard Mark can't watch where he's going! Can you fix it like, right now? Because Daniel is going to rip us if we are late!"

"Yes, of course. Calm down, you have fifteen minutes," I said. Courtney was usually excitable and predictably dramatic as only teenage girls can be.

"It's not a bad tear but I'm going to need some black thread. Let me look in the costume room," I said.

The costume room was on the lower level of the main building which housed the kitchen, dining room, and the great room. The great room was where they held evening worship. The lower level had the costume room, the camp offices, the infirmary and two apartments belonging to the director and assistant director, usually college students.

I hurried down the main staircase shaking my head at Courtney's histrionics, and gratefully admiring Grace's maturity. She had always been quiet and responsible, the kind of student who always helped others and watched out for the kid no one else would play with. Her teachers always told me how they appreciated her sweet spirit. I rounded the corner of the dark corridor and unlocked the costume room with the key ring Shirley had given me. The door creaked open and I was struck by how quiet this floor was.

I guessed everyone was getting ready for the reenactment. I searched for thread for ten minutes before I gave up. It was a long shot but I decided to look in the infirmary. Who knows? Maybe it would turn up there. The long room was divided into three sections, each with a bed and curtain. There was a long countertop with cabinets along the wall and I started opening the cabinet doors to see if there was any thread anywhere. On the third cabinet I came to a metal box with a lock on it. The lock had been sawed in two and when I picked it up it fell to the floor. Wincing at the clatter, I stooped down to pick it up thinking it was some type of medication that had to be locked up.

After all, we were dealing with kids whose whole lives had seen the destruction from drugs, alcohol, and bad choices. Thinking I might find some antihistamine or other medication that could be cooked, sniffed, or otherwise altered I was surprised to find gold coins used in the younger campers' store. The store was set up to reward the kids for good behavior and memorizing bible verses. Grace had told me how they taught the story from the bible in Matthew 17 where Jesus tells the apostles to catch a fish and open its mouth to find gold coins to pay their taxes. The kids loved the story and for many of them and actually some of the counselors it was the first time they had heard it. As I stooped down to pick up the coins and put them back into the box I heard footsteps and Shirley appeared around the door calling out,

"Is anybody in here?" Shirley was in her early 50s and still quite fit and pretty with shiny brown hair and a face framed with spiky bangs. She had incredible energy and displayed a spirit of eternal hope for the camp.

"Yes, Shirley. It's just me, Hope." I said as she entered the room and stared down at the coins.

"What happened? What are those doing in here?" she asked. I explained what I was looking for and what I had found. I watched as she picked up several coins and turned them over in her hands. "But these aren't..." she began and looked up sharply as Daniel, the camp director came into the room.

"Mrs. Stephens, we need the bottles of water for the water truck. Do you know where they are?" he asked. Daniel was tall and built like a lineman with blond hair and dark green eyes.

"Yes, they're in the pantry. There should be 120. One for everyone," I answered.

He crossed over to where we were crouched on the floor picking up the coins. He grabbed the lock and the box.

"Where did this come from?" he asked, his voice angry. I looked up at him with surprise.

"Oh, it's just the kids' reward tokens. I'm sure one of the campers just thought he would keep his stash safe. I guess someone found it, though it looks like this lock has been sawed in two. Kind of scary to think of one of the campers with a saw," I laughed.

"Hope, there should be some black thread in my office drawer. I keep a little sewing kit in there." Shirley said.

"Ok, I guess I better get back. Courtney is afraid you are going to "rip" her, Daniel." I said, pushing myself up off the floor and dusting off my pants.

"No chance, Mrs. Stephens." Daniel said with a smile, one that had caused more than one girl's heart to flutter during his twenty years.

Ch. 3
Hope

The crucifixion reenactment went off without a hitch despite repaired costumes and a few flubbed lines. The campers stood back and watched, their mouths open and tears filling their eyes. They had been too busy with the task of living from day to day to ever phantom what had happened to a lowly carpenter's son on Golgatha. Many of the girls wept, tears flowing down their faces. Two of the girls in Grace's cabin, Stephanie and Jennifer, clung to my hands.

"I just never knew what he went through," Stephanie said, pressing her head against my chest as I hugged her close.

"I know, baby." I said. "But he did and He would do it again, even if you were the only person left on earth."

"No, no I'm worthless. I'm not good for anything," Stephanie sobbed.
"Not so sweet girl, not true at all."

I signaled to the girls' head counselor, a wonderful girl named Susan, and soon Stephanie was surrounded by other campers and staff. Later that night she put on Christ in baptism at the creek while all 120 campers watched. There were 40 kids baptized in all. What a wonderful way to end the day! Stephanie would have a lot to overcome when she returned home. Her past included a mother who was hooked on speed and a father who lost custody of her while in jail for felony drunk driving.

I arrived home exhausted but still flying high from the spiritual joy of seeing so many lives and hearts touched. I came into the kitchen, leafed through the usual bills, and checked the answering machine. There was one message from Shirley.

"Hope, I need to talk to you privately. Can you come to my office after breakfast and ride to town with me? I need to get some things for the scavenger hunt and decorations for the banquet. I want to tell you about something I discovered. Something is not right." she said.

"Something is not right? What is she talking about?" I asked my empty kitchen. Well, whatever it was could wait until morning. I had been on my feet all day and I was exhausted. I enjoyed a hot shower and then related all the events of the day to my wonderful husband, Phillip. He was thrilled to hear of the campers response and also happy to hear that Grace was doing well. We talked for a while then turned out the lights and went to sleep.

I could hardly believe it when the alarm went off. Phillip leaned in close for a kiss. "I made you some coffee." he said and I smiled. We had been married almost 20 years and he still treated me with as much kindness as the first day we met. Not that we didn't have our differences. We did. Phillip headed off to his job in nearby Liberty Hill.

I practically inhaled my coffee on the drive to camp. I rolled my window down to catch the last cool breeze that would be afforded to us on this hot summer day. I pulled into the parking lot at 6:30 a.m., a terrible time to even be awake. However, breakfast for 120 would not be cooked by itself.

I walked up the dirt path and entered the large, air-conditioned kitchen. My two jc's (junior counselors) were waiting to help. This morning we served eggs, bacon, and pancakes. We served the kids family style. Many of them didn't know what it was to eat at a table with napkins, and conversation that didn't include cursing and screaming. With the help of my little team we had the dishes done in no time and the girls went off to their bible studies and activities.

Now it was time to find out exactly what was bothering Shirley. I couldn't imagine what the problem could be, especially that she would want my help with. After so many years of experience the camp ran like a well oiled machine. Shirley was very much the professional, adept at locating government grants and dealing with government agencies. Her parents bought the camp in the seventies. She and her husband, Lance had taken over shortly after they married. She devoted much of her time in the winter months to getting donations and help for the camp.

I entered her office smiling.

"Ok girl, what's up?" I joked.

"Shut the door. Call Bette and have her come in and take over for you for lunch. Meet me at the camp van. Here are the keys. Use your cell from the van. I'll meet you there in ten minutes," Shirley said.

"What? Call Bette? What is up?" I asked laughing.

"Just do it. I'm serious. Please, Hope." she looked at me pleadingly. I felt a ripple of fear and concern. She was obviously upset.

"Ok, ok Shirley. I'll do it. Don't worry about it," I said.

Ten minutes later, after having secured a promise from Bette, I was waiting in the van with the air conditioner running. Shirley came down the sidewalk, a troubled look on her face. She got in the car and fastened her seatbelt. She turned to me and said urgently,

"It's real. The gold. It's real."

"Do what?" I asked.

"The gold. It's not a toy. It's real gold." she said.

"I'm sorry, Shirley. I'm not following you." I said as I pulled out of the parking lot and onto the two lane road to town.

"Remember last night? The gold tokens from the infirmary? It's real. It's real gold," she said.

"Ok... so what does that mean? How could it be real?" I squinted at her in disbelief.

"Do you remember the table, the table in the apartment? Where we had the volunteer orientation?" Shirley asked.

"The table in the apartment? The coffee table? With the money under the glass?" I asked. I remembered the table she was talking about. Several women had commented on how unusual it was. At the time Shirley had explained that the table was kind of a family heirloom. Her father had been a missionary in various countries around the world and he collected foreign monies from each post. She said none of it was very valuable but she couldn't bear to part with it, so she had put it in the apartment.

"Yes, that's the one. Last night, I knew something was wrong. The coins that we picked up from that lockbox were real gold. Have you ever held the tokens? They are very light. There is no way to mistake them by their weight." she said.

"Well, ok so are you saying that your Dad had real gold coins in the table and someone stole them and put them in the lockbox, and then someone else sawed the lock open? And that's what we found last night? What did Daniel think? Did you tell him they were real?" I asked.

By this time we had pulled into the parking lot of the party store by the mall.

"Come on, there is a Starbucks. We can talk there. A little more caffeine won't hurt." I said, trying to lighten the mood and calm her down. It worked for a moment. She was content to go inside the restaurant and order a latte.

We picked a table at the front of the store.

"Did you tell Daniel?" I asked.

"Hope, I think Daniel took them. He stole them from the table. I went to the apartment last night when he was at the reenactment. There are tokens in the table." she was whispering now, the look on her face bordering on frantic.

"Tokens!" she said again.
"Did you talk to Daniel at all about this?" I asked.

"No, I didn't. I wanted to wait until I spoke with Lance. He won't be in until tomorrow. He went to Houston on a fundraising trip. Daniel will pick him up at the airport and they will go straight to the camp because he has a meeting with the board of directors. He'll give a report on how it went in Houston," Shirley said. Her husband, Lance, was a wonderful man and together they had worked tirelessly for Indian Oaks. It was their life. I knew they would be devastated if there was trouble.

"I told Daniel that I would keep the tokens, uh I mean the gold. He knows I have them. I told him I didn't want to encourage the children to hide things," she said.
"Where are they now?" I asked.

"I don't want you to know. If you don't know you can truthfully say you don't," she said.
"How many are there? How much does that translate to? What is gold going for in this crummy economy anyway?" I asked.

"Well, I don't know exactly without calling a bank or a gold broker. What was in the lockbox could translate to possibly a million," she whispered.
"A million dollars!" I shouted.

"Shh!" she hissed, looking around nervously. No one was paying us any attention. We were just two middle aged women out for coffee.
"Oh, ok. Do you think you will file charges against him?" I asked.

"Hope, it breaks my heart. You know he came to camp as a child. He was one of our first campers. I believe it was only the second year that Lance and I were in charge. Then, later he was adopted after his parents' rights were terminated and he worked at the camp, helping to construct the new buildings. He worked for hours each day learning carpentry skills with my Dad."

Richard was a big brawny man whose gentle heart had caused him to devote his life to being a missionary and serving others. I gave her the only advice I could.

"Pray about it. Talk to Lance. Talk to John. Pray some more."

She bowed her head and nodded, tears filling her eyes.

We finished our coffee, talking quietly about the details we still needed to finalize for the banquet. The meat would be provided but I still needed to provide the side dishes. We went to the party store and picked up balloons, crepe paper, and glitter confetti. The banquet was a tradition that had begun during the camp's first year. The counselors wanted to do something nice for the kids to make them feel special. It had worked. The kids woke up on Sunday morning feeling good, and after a rousing morning worship, boarded buses to go back to some of the worst neighborhoods in Dallas and Houston. However, their hearts were forever changed. Not that some didn't still end up in jail, or even dead, but the vast majority of these children were truly changed forever. They had acquired a new friend, Jesus.

One girl had hitchhiked to Shirley in the middle of the night with her 2 year old daughter and had lived with her for a year. Currently, she was going to community college and was about to receive her degree as a nursing assistant.

By the time we ate a light lunch and got back to the camp, it was time for me to prepare dinner. We had 12 visiting sponsors. They were potential donors so we tried to supply them with everything they needed to keep them well fed and comfortable, and also convey an air of professionalism. Shirley and Lance had a dream to build luxury cabins for a bed and breakfast to provide extra income for the camp. One day they would have the resources to do it.

Friday dinner preparations were easy. This was a good thing because after cooking and washing dishes for 120 for a week, I was ready to go home and rest. Dinner was sub sandwiches and bagged chips with chocolate chip cookies for dessert. It was served under a tent in the pasture. The night time worship was held outside. I missed the sound of their beautiful voices lifted up in song while I washed the cookie pans but I was grateful to go home early. I sought out Grace before I left. She was organizing kids into groups but when she saw me she came over to give me a hug.

"Mom, thank you for being here. It means so much."
"Oh, you're welcome, sweetie. If we can help and reach even one of these kids for Jesus it will be worth it." I said. She looked at me then, her beautiful brown eyes filling with tears.

"Mom, I have so much. I am so blessed to have you and Dad." I hugged her again. She had such a tender heart. I placed a kiss on the top of her head.

"I'm going to go, baby. I love you. God bless you." This was always the last thing I said to her at night. I watched the chaos a moment longer as the children were grouped together. I felt a ripple of uneasiness as Daniel came to Grace and announced that they were partners. She looked up at him with a shy smile. If Shirley and Lance decided to press charges against Daniel there could be long term consequences for that young man. Grace was so young I hoped she would not be interested in him.

However, until the Bakers made their decision and confronted Daniel, I felt sure Grace would be safe enough with him in such a big group. The kids were always encouraged not to pair off but to stay in a large, mixed group. Some of the junior counselors that homeschool had chosen courtship practices and being in a group kept the kids safer from temptation. Chaperones added an accountability that I found to be a relief, being the mother of an easily influenced 15 year old.

If only I had intervened and taken her home with me then. After this night, I would not see my baby girl again for six weeks...

Ch. 5
Sat. July 7, 2008
Hope

On Saturday morning I did not miss Grace at breakfast. Sometimes a camper would ask to talk to her at the pavilion or I would just miss her in the rush to get 120 plates and cups filled and then washed. I was grateful the camp kitchen was outfitted with industrial power appliances. I did miss her when the kids exited the dining hall to go to their first bible classes of the day. She always came to me and gave me a hug no matter how busy she was. I thought it was odd but I didn't panic. After all she was 15, not 5. The girl deserved some independence. She had never given her father and I even a moment's worry.

Well now, that's not quite right, there was a time when she was about 18 months old. She left the yard to go and look at the creek on our property while we were experiencing a raging flood. I will never forget the feeling in my heart as I saw her walking back up the hill, covered in mud with a huge smile on her face saying,

"Mama, I go to the cweek!" I could have killed her! Today, I smiled to think of it as I put away the clean pots and pans and began my prep work for lunch. I lost myself in baking snickerdoodle cookies for the campers' morning snack. I love to bake and I was humming a hymn as I put the last of the cookies on a cooling rack.

Courtney entered the kitchen with another young counselor to take the cookies out to the big tent for snack time.

"Mama Stephens, where is Grace? I haven't seen her all day." Courtney asked, a frown on her pretty face.

"What? What do you mean you haven't seen her? She is teaching singing in the pavilion," I said patiently.

"No, we just came from the pavilion." she said pointing to the other counselor.

"Michael had to cover her station because she didn't show up and I asked Stephanie where she was and she said she hadn't seen her all morning. You know Stephanie hasn't left her side since she was baptized the other night." Courtney said.

"That's impossible. You're telling me she missed breakfast and her morning class?"

"When was the last time you spoke to her?" I asked.

"Last night, after the scavenger hunt. She and Daniel were drinking coffee and talking here in the dining hall. I went over and told her goodnight. She said she would come on to the cabin in a few minutes. When I woke up this morning I just thought she got up early to get in a run before it got too hot. She does that sometimes. She and Carmen, that girl from Aggieland," Courtney said.

I knew about her early morning runs. Phillip and I had given her permission as long as she was with someone else. I knew that living with other kids week in and week out got to her sometimes. Being an only child she was used to her privacy. I thought for a moment.

"I'm going to check her cabin. Take the cookies out to the big tent. If Grace is not there, I will go find

Shirley. It's possible she had something for her to do," I said and strode out of the kitchen at a determined pace. Walking down the path my hands began to shake. Surely this was nothing to be concerned about, she had to be here on the campus somewhere. Something had come up was all. I struggled to reassure myself. I prayed as I opened the door to Grace's cabin. My heart fell as I surveyed the dark, empty room. There were no lumps on the beds indicating she was sleeping or sick. I walked over to her bunk, which was neatly made, and picked up her green Nonny bear. She had had Nonny bear since she was four. I saw her tennis shoes arranged neatly under the bed. I knew they were the ones she saved for running. They were the new kind that allowed more air to circulate. I stared at them for a minute, my face flushing and my heart began to pound.

Don't panic, I told myself. Go find Shirley. It took effort but I got my feet moving and I ran back to the main building and down the big staircase to Shirley's office. It was locked and dark. I walked down the corridor and knocked on Daniel's door. He came to the door of his apartment wearing a swim suit, Tshirt, and flip flops.

"Mrs. Stephens, what can I do for you?" he asked politely.
"Have you seen Grace this morning?" I asked urgently.

"Why no, I haven't. I was just spending some time alone preparing my final sermon for the banquet. I promised to take some of the younger boys fishing off the pier." he said. He closed the door behind him and locked it with a key he pulled from his pocket.

"Grace did not show up for breakfast or morning classes. I went to her cabin and she wasn't there. I was afraid she was sick. Do you know where Shirley is?" I asked.

Daniel cleared his throat, a pained look on his face. "Um, Mrs. Stephens, I know this isn't what you want to hear, but some of the senior counselors were talking about going to Sixth Street last night. She might have gone with them after we had coffee together." he said.

Sixth Street was in downtown Austin. It was an area of bars, live music, and loose morals. The senior counselors were all college students over 18. "My daughter would never have gone there! She's 15 years old." I snapped. "Where is Mrs. Baker?"

"She called in sick, had a virus or something. Lance should be in later today. I will pick him up from the airport at 3:00." he said.
"Please let me know if you see Grace," I ordered and turned on my heel. I stomped up the stairs, my mind whirling. Where could she be? I put a hand in my pocket and brought out my cell phone. I tried Grace first, leaving a frantic voice mail telling her to call me if she knew what was good for her. Next, I tried Phillip and left a message on his cell asking him to call me about Grace's schedule. I didn't want to scare him, at least not when she could walk in any moment.

What should I do now? I stood outside the great room, a weight on my chest keeping me from taking a deep breath. Think, Hope, think.

"Mrs. Stephens?" a voice said to my right. It was Madison, the assistant director, whose apartment was also downstairs.
"Is everything ok?"she asked. "The jcs who are on

KP duty want to know what to do about lunch. I told them I would try to track you down," she said. Her long, carrot red hair streamed over her shoulders and I noticed how it shined in the light of the sunny room. I took a deep breath finally, and said, "Grace is gone. No one has seen her today and Daniel thinks she went to Sixth Street last night."

"Grace? Oh no, I don't think so. The only ones that I know of that ended up going were Kyle and Steve. I can't imagine Grace going with them." she shook her head and frowned.

"But where could she be? Michael said she didn't show up for her singing station in the pavilion and he had to cover for her. Courtney said Stephanie hadn't seen her in the cabin before breakfast. Shirley called in sick. I don't know what to do," I said helplessly. I jumped as my cell phone rang in my pocket. It was Phillip.

"Hi, honey. What's up with Grace's schedule and how much is it going to cost me?" he joked.
"I don't want to scare you, honey but I think Grace is missing. She has not been seen by anyone since last night. Some of the kids went to Sixth Street." I said gravely. There was a long pause. I could hear him breathing and a sob caught in my throat. More than anything I yearned to feel his calming presence and his warm hand in mine.

"Can you come out here?" I asked, my voice breaking.
"Call the police. I'm leaving now." he said abruptly and broke the connection. I closed my eyes and prayed for his safety. Madison was looking at me with a scared expression.

"Mrs. Stephens, we have a procedure for this kind of thing," she said.

"A procedure?" I asked.

"Yeah, like when I worked at Walmart? They call a Code Adam and lock down the exits and every associate has to look for the lost kid. We had a kid run away from camp last year," she said.
"What happened to him?" I asked absently.

"Oh, he was fine. He came in about dinner time. He was sunburned and covered in mosquito and ant bites. He was dehydrated but very glad to be back in civilization." she laughed. "I will go and begin our procedure and you can go ahead and call the police." She turned to go, the sound of her flip flops echoing in the great room.

"Dear God," I prayed. "Grace is my only child. You gave your only child for me and my sins. Please, please..." I moaned to myself and rested my head on the wall for support. I didn't know what else to pray for. Panic made my mind blank.

Ch. 6
Hope

Hope, you've got to get yourself together, I thought. If I can just hold it together until Philip gets here everything will be ok. I braced myself and walked into the kitchen and dialed 911. I explained the information about Grace and when she was last seen and her height and clothes for 25 minutes until they finally agreed to send an officer out to the camp. In the meantime, I made a pot of coffee just for something to do. I was vaguely aware of the huge crowd of campers gathering in the dining hall to pray for Grace and divide into search groups. I breathed a sigh of relief when I saw two officers stride into the building. They walked with authority and confidence.

"Hope?" said the tall, mustached, officer.

He reached out his hand and I took it and squeezed it. It was Kenneth Glenn. We had worshipped together for years at the little white rock church in town. Our church was a sponsor for the camp. At a time like this, I was very grateful to live in a small town. It was so different from the coastal town I had grown up in.

"When I heard it was Grace I asked for the case. I called the prayer chain. Is Philip on his way?" he asked.

"Yes. I am so glad you are here." I said.

"Have a seat. This is Officer Hodge. He has transferred to us from San Antonio. His daughter is at U.T." he said and I looked at him for the first time. He was short and balding with a pleasant smile.

"Mrs. Stephens, I want you to know we are going to do everything in our power to bring Grace home today. It is very unlikely that anything has happened to her. In 90 percent of all cases these kids are home by evening." Officer Hodge said.

I gave him a bland smile but said nothing. Ken grabbed a cup and poured me some coffee. We went through the motions of cream and sugar, then Ken began to take down Grace's information. Height, weight, etc. He was explaining how an Amber Alert was issued when Philip came in. I ran into his arms and cried for the first time. When I got myself together the men shook hands and made introductions to Officer Hodge. I poured Philip a glass of iced tea and we sat down together holding hands.

"We need a recent picture of Grace," Officer Hodge said. "There is one on the bulletin board, in the hallway," I said.

The foyer of the dining hall displayed photos of each counselor. I walked to the foyer and took down the smiling picture. I stared at it while I prayed then handed it over to Officer Hodge.

"Her hair was shorter then. She had just gotten a haircut. It's longer now," I babbled on.
"It's ok, Hope," Ken said gently.

"Ok, folks. We need to get this Amber Alert issued. You need to call your extended family. It's possible someone has heard from her. You don't want your family to hear about this on the news. The media coverage will be intense. As irritating as they can be, they are also our best ally in getting the information out to the public." Hodge finished his speech and shook our hands, still offering reassurances.

Ken guided us into the dining room where the search groups were coming inside to rest and get water. He spoke with Daniel, Madison, and John Baker who had heard about the search and joined in. Ken came back to us with a shake of his head.

"Nothing yet, but that's good news. She's going to come waltzing in here in just a moment. Don't you worry," he said.

We didn't even pretend to answer. John walked up to Philip and shook his hand. "She's got to be here somewhere. She's such a good little girl." he said, his brown eyes filling with tears.
"I've decided to cancel the banquet," he said.

"No, John. Don't do that. The kids look forward to the banquet all week. They have already given up their morning classes to look for Grace. Plus, Lance has that report to give to the board about the fundraising trip. Don't cancel that, too. The camp business must go on as usual," I pleaded.

"I agree with Hope, John. Don't call it off," Philip said. I turned to look at him and he put his arm around me. "Well, ok then, if you're sure. Lance will help when he arrives. I am going to look for Daniel." he said.

Officer Ken came to us then and said, "Who was the last person to see Grace last night?"
"Daniel. They had coffee together in the dining room," I replied. "What do you know about him?" he asked pulling out his black notebook.
"Oh, I don't think…" I shook my head.
"What is his last name?" he asked.
"Well, it used to be Ferguson. He was adopted by a couple named Johnson about 10 years ago.
He was about 14 at the time. Uh… actually I do know a little bit more but I don't want to break

a confidence until I speak with Shirley," I said hesitantly. Ken stared hard at me.

"Break it. Now is not the time to protect anyone. If there is anything I need to know to help find your daughter I'm going to use it," he spoke forcefully.

"Let's go somewhere more private to talk," I said looking at Philip nervously. Ken escorted us into the kitchen and we closed the doors. The big room glistened with stainless steel appliances and bright overhead lights.

"Ok, Thursday night I was in the infirmary looking for thread to mend a costume, and ..." I began.

"You were looking for thread in the infirmary?" Philip interrupted.

"It doesn't matter. I found a lock box that had been sawed open. It was full of gold coins. I thought they were the campers tokens they use in the reward store. Shirley and Daniel came in and I showed them. The next day Shirley confided to me that they were real gold coins worth at least a million dollars that she suspects Daniel stole from the apartment he is staying in. The coins came from a glass topped table that her father owned. It was full of money from his missionary trips abroad."

I finished and sat down in a chair. Suddenly, I was exhausted. My brain felt fuzzy and I didn't know what to think anymore.

"Did she know? Did she know the coins were real?" Philip asked.

"She thought they were just foreign coins. It was an heirloom, a reminder of her father. She couldn't bear to part with it. You remember how close she was to her father. He came and preached out here for a few years after he came back to the states. He and John got along famously. Richard helped out here with the construction of the new buildings before he retired," I said.

"Didn't he die last year? Had cancer?" Ken asked. "Yes, he did." I replied.

"So she thinks Daniel stole the coins from the table?" Ken asked.

"Yes, she checked and the coins in the table are tokens. Listen, I feel really bad telling you about this without Shirley's permission," I said.

"Where is Shirley anyway? She's usually racing around here with a whistle around her neck and a clipboard."

"She's sick. I didn't want to bother her until she is better. We went to lunch yesterday and she was really upset."

"Ok, I am going to talk to Hodge about this. We will keep the details quiet and do some background checks. You both need to get on the phone and notify your extended families. The Amber Alert for Grace will be issued at 6 pm. If we don't hear anything from her by 9 pm, I want to get it on the 10 o'clock news. Philip, I will want you to make a statement," Ken said, stepping from friend back into police officer mode. The door closed behind him, and Philip pulled me to my feet. I looked at him and he hugged me.

"Ok, now we need to get those calls made. Do you want me to do it?" he asked.
"Where is she? Where could she be?" I began to cry again. Philip held me close and waited. When I got myself together he asked if I had eaten anything. I told him I didn't think I could swallow anything. He made me eat a piece of fruit and then we went down to Shirley's office to make our calls.

Philip called his parents in Tennessee. They were alarmed but said they would be praying every second until they heard Grace was safe. He called his sister and aunt in Austin. His sister was still at work but his aunt said she would pray and start canvassing the Sixth Street area. We didn't think this was a very good idea but we couldn't discourage her.

Now it was my turn. I had grown up on the coast in Port Aransas. My parents had been killed in a car accident while I was in college. After that, my Aunt Ruth moved in with me while I finished my degree. She was my mother's only sister and we had coped with our grief by cooking. While we cooked, she would tell me stories about our family. She still lived in the little house I grew up in. I spoke with Ruth and told her not to panic, that an Amber Alert would be issued but we really thought she had just had a late night out with friends and would be in any minute. I don't think she believed me but I promised to call her the very second we saw Grace. She ended her call with, "God Bless you" just like I have always said to Grace.

When we had finished making our calls, Philip said he needed to get some air and wanted to check and see how the search was coming. We walked back up the stairs and I ran into Bette. She opened her arms to me and gave me a fierce hug. No words were necessary. She sat with me in the kitchen and after an hour we began to work on dinner. The 6 pm deadline was coming fast. Grace, where are you? My mind stayed mostly numb. I had not let myself wonder about where she could be or what could be happening to her.

Ch. 7
Hope

     At 5:30 Lance walked into the kitchen. He carried enormous platters of smoked meat and the rich smell that normally made me swoon made me feel ill.

"Hope, Officer Ken says he's ready for you. The news people are here and they want to issue the Amber Alert for the 6 pm news," he said.

     "Ok. Have you talked to Shirley since you've been home?" I asked.

 "I called but just got the machine. She's probably sleeping. Her allergies are always bad during the summer and when you put a virus on top of that I'm sure she's sleeping it off. I'll take off tomorrow to tend to her when Grace is home safe and sound." he said giving me a warm smile.

     I walked into the dining hall and looked around with a heavy heart. The room looked beautiful, completely transformed into an elegant ballroom. The crepe paper and helium balloons made it festive and the tablecloths and flowers were so pretty. Grace should be here tending to her campers. She always loved the banquet. This year her dress was an emerald green color and it complimented her brown hair so beautifully.

     "God, please help her…" I whispered to the emptiness.

     I managed to get through the Amber Alert. We didn't have to say anything the authorities just wanted us there in the hopes that maybe Grace would see us and come home on her own.

I forced myself to serve at the banquet. It kept my mind off of Grace and gave me something to do. It felt right to stay here with the other campers. When she came back I wanted her to know that I was here. If only I had known how close she really was…

About 9 pm, after the banquet was over and I was still washing dishes, the doors opened and Philip and Ken walked in.

"It's time, honey," Philip said. I took a deep breath, folded my apron and took his hand. He put his arm around me and we walked into the foyer of the great room where microphones had been set up and news people crowded around. Philip made his prepared speech and although I shed a few tears I was able to join him in asking the public for their help and Grace to please call home. I felt as though my heart was being seared with a hot iron. After the news people left and the campers held one last prayer for Grace's safety, Ken suggested we go home.

"If you are up to it, I would like to come by in a few minutes to search her room. Since she disappeared from the camp that's why we have concentrated our efforts around here today but I think it is time we search her room. We have been monitoring her Facebook account and her cell and have not gotten anywhere. We are waiting for background checks on some of the staff and counselors. Have you seen Daniel lately?" he asked. I looked blankly at Philip.

"No, he brought Lance back to camp and then said he was going to search some trails he knew of she might have taken for a run. Daniel never came back. Madison had to conduct the banquet and did a great job."

Philip said, "Listen Ken, I want to get Hope home, she looks all done in. Come by whenever you want. I need to get her home." He put his arm around me and led me out to the car. I was so ready to be at home.

We pulled in the driveway, and for a moment my heart leapt thinking maybe she had spent the day holed up in her room. I raced through the yard fence and was met by Grace's dog, Sam. I petted her and she whined against me feeling my anxiety as her own. I let her in the door ahead of me, suddenly dreading the silence I knew would come. I walked into the kitchen to check the machine.

"Honey, let me do that. Go upstairs and take a hot shower. Ken will be here in a few minutes and I know you aren't going to get any sleep tonight. Take a few minutes to yourself, you'll feel better. We'll spend the rest of the time in prayer."

His deep voice was so soothing I leaned my head against his chest and closed my eyes. All I wanted to do was open my eyes and see my daughter before me. Reluctantly, I trudged up the stairs and ran a hot shower. I removed my clothes and was about to step in the shower when Philip pounded on the door.

"Hope, get down here! You need to hear this!" he shouted.

"What? What! Is it her? Is it Grace?" I screamed, and snatched up my bathrobe. I raced down the stairs, falling the last few steps.

"It's Shirley. Listen," Philip said and switched on the answering machine. Her voice was just above a whisper and I had to strain to hear her.

"Hope? Hope can you hear me? It's Shirley. It's about 7 am Saturday, and Daniel is here. He says he wants to talk about the coins without the police being involved. I told him I would make some coffee. Could you come over? I'm kind of scared to be alone with him. The gold coins are buried under the rock house."

The line was strangely silent then I gasped and tears entered my eyes as I heard Shirley scream,

"No please! Daniel, dear God, no!" She began to sob and the line went dead.

I looked at Philip, the horror on his face matching my own. The doorbell rang and Sam immediately started barking. I jumped and wrapped my arms around my middle. Philip went to answer the door and I sank down in a kitchen chair. I prayed for Shirley. I prayed for Daniel. I just wanted this day to end and to hold my daughter. I feared nothing in my life would ever be the same after this day. I was right...

Officer Ken came into the kitchen and listened to the tape. He immediately called Officer Hodge to go to Lance and Shirley's house. He said that as long as he was here he would search Grace's room. I sat motionless in my chair while the men were upstairs. The phone began to ring. I ran to it and snatched it up. "Grace?" I said.

"Hope?" a man's voice began to sob. It was a horrible sound. I felt my stomach drop and a sickness filled me.

"Shirley is dead. There is blood everywhere." It was Lance and he was weeping into the phone harsh, pitiful sounds. I let the phone fall to the floor.

"Oh, Lord please help me. Please help me." For a moment I wasn't sure if the voice was Lance or myself. I began to scream for Philip. He ran into the kitchen, Ken with him, his hand on his holster. Philip picked up the phone. Strangely, everything went black and when I woke up I was on my couch with an afghan over me. Philip was leaning over me.

"Ken went to Lance's. Shirley is dead. Hodge called. They think it must have been Daniel," he said.

"Oh…" I groaned. "If only I had been here this morning I could have helped her," I said.

"You could have been killed as well. They are putting out an APB on Daniel right now." Philip smoothed my hair back from my forehead. The phone rang again.

"What now?" Philip moaned. I grabbed for the remote phone located between our recliners.
"It could be Grace," I said.

"Hello?"

"Are you listening?" a calm, deep voice said.
"What? Yes! Who is this?" I squinted trying to hear. He spoke again, calmly and deliberately.

"Are you listening?" It was Daniel.
"Daniel, is that you?" I asked, clutching at Philip's shirtsleeve. He sat up quickly and I shared the phone with him so he could hear.

"Are you listening?" he asked again.
"Yes! Yes, what do you have to say?" I replied frantically.

"I have Grace. I want the gold. Go get it and bring it to me. When I get it back, you can have Grace back. I haven't hurt her. Not yet."

"Let me talk to her," I begged. I heard shuffling and then Grace's voice,

"Mom?" her voice sounded hoarse like she had been crying. Then the line went dead.

Philip took the phone from me and hung it up. "Get dressed!" he said. I just stared at him. "Move!" he shouted. His harsh tone got me moving and I knew what I had to do. Moving quickly, I ran upstairs and dressed in jeans, and tennis shoes. I found two flashlights and raced down the stairs.

"Let's go," I said. He grabbed his keys and we piled into his truck. I noticed he had loaded a shovel and a pick.

"Where is the rock house?" he asked.

"At the camp, in the older section by the tank."

"I've never heard of the rock house," he said.

"They don't call it that anymore because of the drug reference. Now they call it the creekside cottage."

He peeled out of our driveway and headed down the street spraying gravel. I braced myself and reached for my seatbelt.

"What did she mean by saying it was under the rock house? There is nothing under the rock house," I said.

"How old is the building?" Phillip asked thoughtfully.

"Old. It's one of the original buildings," I answered.

"Well, a lot of these old rock buildings have a crawl space underneath them. I know the dining hall has a huge one they deliberately put there for storage. I went under it when I wired up the apartments," he said.

I had forgotten that he had done the electric for the additional apartments. The gravel made a crunching sound under the truck tires as we turned into the camp. We took the road as far as possible and walked the rest of the way to the rock house.

"Oh, honey, should we have called Ken or Hodge?" I asked, fear making my stomach hurt.

"No, I don't think so. They have their hands full with Lance, and Shirley's death. Besides, we have to do whatever we can to bring Grace home as soon as possible. Daniel has killed once, and the longer she stays with him the more dangerous it is for her. We can't worry about anyone else right now," He sounded adamant and his confidence made me feel better. We were at the rock house now and Philip leaned down and looked at the underside of the porch.

"Yeah, it's pier and beam. Lots of these old buildings are. I'll crawl under here and look. Let's hope she's marked it in some way."

He slid out of sight and I prayed he would find it with ease. I stood quietly in the dark feeling the warm wind blowing over me and listening to the sound of crickets chirping. After a few minutes of shoveling he came huffing out from under the building.

"She marked it all right, with a rubber fish. What was that about?" he asked.

I thought for a second, exhaustion making my mind slow. "Oh right, the kids learn a scripture story about Jesus paying taxes with money. It's found in Matthew 17," I said, smiling to think that Shirley remembered.

Tears welled in my eyes when I thought she had been alive just yesterday and we had prayed together. Then she had crawled under this very building. Now I was fighting to save my daughter from the person who took her life. My mind was swirling with questions. Where was Grace? How were we going to get her back?

"How much did she say this is worth?" Philip asked, hefting the bag under his arm.

"Shirley thought it might be a million dollars," I said quietly.

"Let's get out of here. We need to get back home in case he contacts us again. He may be watching us." Philip said and I felt a cold chill run down my back.

Ch. 8
Hope

Within a half hour we were back in our kitchen with the gold coins laying sparkling on our dining table. "What do we do now?" Philip asked.

"We wait," I said.

"No, I mean what do we do when Daniel calls and wants to make the exchange?" he asked and I could see he was deep in thought.

"We cooperate. Tell him we'll do whatever he wants us to," I said. "What do you want to do, call in the police? Call Hodge and Ken?" I asked.

"Daniel has already killed once. He knows that you, Grace, and I know that he stole the gold. He's got to know that we have already told the police about that. What is to keep him from killing Grace or us?" Philip asked.

"Honey, what are you saying?" I asked, panicked.

"I'm just thinking. If we give him the gold, what kind of leverage do we have to get Grace back? He's got the gold, then off he goes. He could do anything then," he said. I stared at him with my mouth open.

"If we hid the gold from him then we could spend the time looking for Grace and then he's under our thumb, he has to come on our terms, deliver what we want. We make it so he has to keep Grace safe in order to get the gold back."

"You are talking about our child!" I shouted. "I want her back tonight. I don't care what he does with the money!" I cried.

"I know, I know just hear me out. I'm trying to be smart. We have to be careful and take the best chance of getting her back safely. I think this is it. You take the coins and hide. I will track him down and bring Grace home," Philip said.

I stared at him, unbelieving. "You're crazy. You are bargaining with our child's life," I said. "Meanwhile, she's still gone. Every minute she spends with him endangers her life, but you've got to ask yourself, what he will do when he gets the money? What if he never even tells us where she is and he leaves her somewhere to die?" he asked, his voice breaking.

"Stop it!" I shouted. We both began to cry and reached for each other. We sank down on the floor. The sound of our sorrow permeated our silent house.

"We need a plan," I finally said, sniffing. "I think you should take the money and hide it. Then run somewhere and hide yourself. Meanwhile, I will get Grace back and we will let the police take care of the rest," Philip said.

"Where am I supposed to go? How are you going to be able to get Grace back?" I asked. "When he no longer has access to the coins he will contact us. Somehow I'll make it work. I will find her and bring her home. I promise you."

He sounded so determined I believed he really could. "I'll tell everyone that Grace called and she hitchhiked to Memphis to see my folks. I'll tell them we all had a fight and we didn't want anyone to know. I will say that you have flown up there to spend some time with them, talk it out and bring Grace home before school starts. That will satisfy the Amber Alert, the police and the camp. Now, where can you go to hide the money?" he asked.

We considered several possibilities. It was almost midnight when the perfect solution came to mind. I had been praying for wisdom and the Lord provided it.

"Philip, do you remember me telling you about my prom night?" I asked. He gave me a wary look, then understanding dawned on his face.

"It's perfect," he said.

I had spent my prom night on Carolina Key. It was a fun, high school dare. Carolina Key is a tiny, uninhabited island off the coast of Port Aransas. Every hour during the day, a jetty boat brings tourists back and forth to the island with their children, ice chests full of fried chicken, and dogs. There is nothing on the island, not even a bathroom. It is only two miles long. Some people come to see the unpolluted beach and to look for shells and starfish early in the morning. Some people come to swim and have a great ocean experience with their kids. It is beautiful and unspoiled.

We had gone on a dare to spend the night. There were four of us, two couples. My boyfriend Brad, my best friend Elizabeth and her boyfriend Alex. We all attended the Church of Christ in Port Aransas together. Another friend named Shawna had issued the dare one day at lunch. We took her up on it and were successful. We had each ridden out on separate jetty boats and then buried ourselves in the sand. When night fell we waited for the security guard to make a run through on his four wheeler. As soon as he left we knew we were safe.

Alex had buried some food the day before. Nothing fancy, just crackers and things. It was a beautiful night under the stars.

"It's perfect," Philip said again. "Ok, we need to prepare. You must lay down for a while. I know you won't sleep, but you've got to be awake enough to drive down to Port Aransas. You need to pack a bag. Let's say you'll leave the house at 5 am. I will call Ken at 6 am and tell him that my parents called and you are flying to Memphis. I'll call Aunt Ruth and the rest of the family and tell them the same thing."

Philip took my arm and helped me upstairs. My head was spinning, but it felt good to have a plan. Philip set the alarm for 5 am. We lay down on our bed, held each other close, and prayed together. I closed my eyes and I guess I must have dozed because I heard the alarm go off.
Philip shut it off and rolled over saying,

"I'll go make some coffee. It's going to be a long day."
I sensed a sadness and fatigue about him that wasn't there yesterday. I sat up in bed, covered my face with my hands and whispered,

"Where are you Grace?" I prayed for her then, and for Lance. I also prayed for Daniel but it didn't come easy and I had to force myself to do it. I dressed quickly, grabbed my bags and hurried downstairs. Philip was waiting with a hot cup of coffee and a wrapped sandwich. I was amazed at the kindness and thoughtfulness he showed me even at a time like this. He truly lived out the scripture in Ephesians 5:25.

"I found an old brochure from one of our trips to Carolina Key. You should be able to make the 2 pm jetty boat. Stop and buy some Gatorade so you don't get dehydrated. Don't attract any attention to yourself. You need to be buried and in position by 4 pm. The last boat is at 5 and the security guard should make his round by 4 wheeler by 6 at the latest. After that you can come out. Stay alert for any boats that may be able to spot you. Stay in the brush as much as possible. Try to get some sleep," Philip said.

He handed me a child's purple sand bucket.

"What is this for?" I laughed. I looked inside it at the gold coins.

"It won't look suspicious on the island," he responded. "I stole it from the kid next door. Bury the bucket and the coins. The first boat of the morning is at 8 am. Remember to stay hidden until the beach is well populated. Take the 8:30 or 9:00 jetty boat back to the car." He took my hand and helped me out the door and into the car. He hugged me long and hard and kissed me.

"Tomorrow, drive to Corpus Christi and stock up on supplies, get cash. Drive to Hot Springs, Arkansas. I'll make you a reservation at the KOA. We've stayed there before and it is nice and safe. Wait for me. Grace and I will come to you."
We stared at each other for a long time.

"I promise you, Hope. I'm going to find her and bring her home."
I nodded and asked, "What are you going to do?"

"I'm going to tell him he's going to have to follow my instructions on returning Grace," he said.
My eyes filled with tears as I started the engine.

"Godspeed," he whispered as I pulled out of the driveway.

Ch. 9
Sun. July 8, 2008
Philip

I watched Hope pull from the driveway. The bright sun was shining, and the wind blew cool as I stared at the car disappearing around the corner.

"Time to move," I said. I turned quickly and headed inside. I was formulating a plan and it was time to act. I called Ken and was put through right away. He sounded out of breath.

"Hello, Philip. I was just organizing the search of the tank out at the camp. Have you heard anything?" he asked.

"Yes, actually I have. We talked to Grace last night. She hitchhiked to my folks up in Memphis. Hope flew out this morning to stay a few days and bring Grace home before school starts. We had a little fuss and were a little embarrassed to tell anyone. I guess it's just typical teenage stuff. I do want to thank you and your team for all your help and support and to offer you an apology for all the trouble we've caused the department," I said.

He paused for a moment and I squirmed, hoping he believed me. He cleared his throat.
"Well... Philip, that's what we're here for. I'm delighted that you've heard from her. We are always anxious for a positive outcome. Hitchhiking, though? That doesn't sound like Grace. That kid is solid as a rock, always has been. Is there anything you are not telling me? Anything you'd care to keep off the record?" he asked.

"No, Ken. Nothing like that." I was quick to reassure him.

"Well, in that case I will go and cancel the Amber Alert and let the dive team go. I'll be keeping you all in my prayers," Ken said.

"Thanks a lot. I appreciate it." I hung up then, so relieved this part was over.

Ken was a great policeman and an even better friend. I was a little scared he would see through my story. I was walking out the back door when the phone rang again.

"Hello?" I said.

"Are you listening?" It was Daniel.

"Yes, I'm listening. Are you? Are you listening good?" I gripped the phone in my fist, suddenly allowing some of the anger I felt to reach the surface.

"I'm going to tell you how this game is going to be played. You are a low life coward who took the life of a woman who tried to help children change their lives. You had better hope that my daughter sleeps well tonight. You better hope that she eats well because if anything happens to her you will never see a single gold coin. You had better bring my daughter home, and I mean right now. The gold is gone, out of reach for you and even for me. When Grace is safely home then, and only then, will I deliver the gold to you. You see, you made a mistake letting us get the gold first. Now you must do it my way. I want to talk to my daughter." I finished then, wiping the sweat from my brow. Daniel had remained silent the whole time. I had to wonder if I was endangering Grace, given Daniel's instability and violent tendency.

"Daddy?" I bowed my head and closed my eyes, pinching the skin between my eyes to stop the tears from coming. Joy flooded my soul just hearing her sweet voice.

"It's going to be ok, baby. I'm going to bring you home. Everything is going to be fine," I said as calmly as I could. I desperately wanted to reassure her. I took a breath to ask if she was ok, and did she need anything when the line went dead. I sighed in frustration. I had to figure out where he was holding her. It almost certainly had to be somewhere at or near the camp. I needed information. Who was Daniel and why would he do this? Where did this gold come from? How had Shirley's Dad acquired it? I needed answers and there was only one place to get them.

I headed out on the road to the camp. I wanted to call Hope and tell her about the call but that would have to wait. Lance and Shirley lived on the camp property but had a separate driveway. Their house was a beautiful two story log cabin with four gabled windows.   I estimated that it was about 1/2 a mile from there to the dining hall. That would have made it very convenient for Daniel to sneak back and forth without being seen. Even if someone had seen him on the trail, no questions would be asked. Just out for a walk.

I turned into Lance's driveway and stopped the car. Lance opened the door before I knocked and I wondered if he had been hoping someone would come. I knew that in a matter of hours his house would be filled with members of his family and our church. No one grieves alone.
We were a tight knit little community and everyone came together when needed. I reached out my hand for a handshake and he took it, then fell against my shoulder, crying. I bit my lip and pounded him on

the back, the equivalent of a man-hug. I tried not to cry myself but failed. The man who killed the love of his life had my daughter. I prayed silently for Lance.

I prayed for Grace and Hope. We walked into the house and into the kitchen. He didn't say a word, just poured me a cup of coffee and sat down at the table. We sat in silence for a while and then I asked, "How are the kids?"

He shook his head and smiled. "As good as can be expected. I am worried about Janie. She is just out of college. She needs her mother the most right now. Ben and Debra will be here in a few hours. Little B.J. will be with them. I can't wait to see him, get my hands on him. Shirley loved him so. He turned one year old last week. To lose her like this..." His voice trailed off and he pulled out his handkerchief and blew his nose. It suddenly occurred to him and he asked about Grace. I told him my made up story and he said he was very relieved that she was ok.

"She's a good girl, y'all have done a good job raising her. She'll come around soon enough."

"I appreciate the thought, it's mostly Hope's doing. She's been a great mother," I said. I could tell that in his grief, the information didn't quite soak in. The telephone rang just then, and I decided to take advantage of the situation. I waved to the hallway and he nodded his consent. I walked down the hall and turned the bathroom light on. I turned on the faucet in the sink, then continued down the hall to the back door. It sounded like he was speaking to someone from church or the camp. There was a laundry room on the right and a rack of keys was mounted beside the door. I searched through them until I found a set labeled camp. I lifted it off, slipped it into my pocket and hurried back to the bathroom. After a moment I came back to the table. Lance was sitting alone, staring out the window. He seemed glad to see me.

"That was Susan. The counselors and staff have organized a prayer service tonight at 6:00. They want to offer their support and wishes. Will you be able to come? I'd like for you to be there," he said.

"Sure, Lance. I'll be there. In fact I thought I would head out there right now to get Grace's stuff and attend worship. Do you need anything? Is there anything I can do for you before I leave?" I asked. He shook his head. I could tell he didn't have any idea what he should do, at all. At the moment, he was truly a lost soul. We said our goodbyes and I prayed for him as I drove the short distance to the dining hall and parked.

The worship service was beautiful. I asked to lead the first prayer and took the opportunity to make an announcement that Grace had contacted us and was safely in Memphis with my parents. Her friends shed tears of relief that she was safe. The mood in the service was bittersweet, rejoicing over Grace's safety, yet sorrowful for Shirley's loss and her grieving family. John offered a prayer of thanksgiving for the many who had given the family their support. He left as soon as the service was over to be with Lance.

Most of the young people had concluded that the murder was the act of an intruder. I was sure the police would not give out more information than they thought necessary. Daniel's absence was noticed. He normally led the service and gave one last sermon to the campers before they got on the bus to go back home to their families. Usually he had them so pumped up they sang all the way home. Where could he be was the question on everyone's mind, especially at a time when the camp needed him the most to pray together and get them through Shirley's death.

When the service was over I found Susan and asked for permission to go to the cabin to pick up Grace's belongings. I was banking on the fact that Daniel hadn't gone far and would have some way of keeping up with what was going on at the camp.

I went straight to Grace's cabin, and using a trash bag I found in the bathroom, I emptied all of her belongings into it. I walked back to the truck and tossed it in the back seat. I doubted there was anything that would lead me to her in her belongings. I could always go through them later. I tried to eliminate all the buildings that were high traffic areas. I went to the rock house and checked it all over. I had brought a ladder and I put it up against the outer wall. I walked around on the roof. There was no attic. The building was empty. I checked under the building where we found the gold last night. In the light of day, the space was small and cramped and there was nothing out of the ordinary. In the small space I managed to turn myself over, scraping my elbows and knees to check the underside of the building. Aside from the lipstick words reading "Denny loves Latrice" there was nothing of interest.

I crawled out and dusted myself off. My cell phone rang in my pocket. I looked at the screen but I didn't recognize the number. I flipped it open and said hello.

"Do you have the gold?" Daniel asked.
"I told you the gold will be yours once I get Grace

back, and not before," I replied tersely.

The line hummed with silence and then went dead.

He doesn't know what to do now, I thought.

It was more important than ever to find Grace immediately. Who knows what he might do? Keeping Grace from harm was my first responsibility. He had to be around the camp somewhere. He had to have access to food, phone and information. I wondered if he was close enough to be watching me. I sighed with frustration. I wanted to tear this camp up and everything in it. It was almost empty and this was my best chance to make a thorough search of
all the buildings. Most of the counselors had gone to Austin to eat lunch and enjoy themselves, going to movies or out to play golf. They would be back tonight for the prayer service. On Monday afternoon they would receive a new batch of campers.

I spent the next two hours searching the storage buildings under the dining hall. I found nothing. I walked wearily into the main building and after resting for a few moments I decided to try downstairs. I looked through Shirley's office and searched the closets in the costume room. I looked around in the infirmary and saw a door I had not noticed before. I opened it and gasped at what I found. On the floor of the closet was a bundle of duct tape, a crushed can of Diet Mountain Dew and a ring of Grace's. Diet Mountain Dew was Grace's favorite drink. She was famous for it. The ring was one I had given her myself. It was a purity ring with the words, "true love waits". On her 14th birthday, I took her out to the Olive Garden and talked with her about the decision she had made to court rather than date. Many of her peers were choosing this option over the temptations of dating. I wanted to make sure that she was committed to it before I gave her the ring. Inside I was squirming, I hated talking about this kind of stuff and felt my palms grow sweaty anytime a sensitive subject came up. I had whined to Hope, "Do we have to talk about this stuff? I used to just take her for ice cream and teach her how to catch a decent pop fly." She just smiled and nodded.

I took the ring and put it on my pinky. It barely fit. I felt myself tear up. Be safe, Grace. I thought. Lord, keep her safe. My phone rang again...

Ch. 10
Sun. July 8, 2008
Hope

I gritted my teeth and tried not to cry as I pulled down the driveway. I soon gave up and let all the pent up emotions drain from me. My sobs filled the car for a long time. When I was able to take a deep breath and wipe the tears from my cheeks, I began to pray. At first I'm sure the Lord had a hard time figuring out my ramblings but I prayed my heart to him anyway.

Heading south down 281 was an easy drive, one I had made many times to visit Aunt Ruth both by myself, and with Philip and Grace. I wished I had had time to talk to Aunt Ruth. She was such a strong woman and so full of faith. I would have to try to call her tomorrow night but I couldn't possibly let her know anything was wrong or it could put her in danger. The miles passed quickly and I enjoyed the cool air from the air conditioner. I knew that once I was buried in the sand I was going to be hot. Philip was right. I couldn't afford to become dehydrated. I stopped at a convenience store when I got to San Antonio and filled a bag with sandwiches for lunch and dinner and a six pack of Gatorade. Except for a fast pit stop, I wouldn't stop again.

When I arrived in Port Aransas I took the ferry across the bay, feeling sorry for the men and women working traffic on the ferry landing. That was such a hot job. After I pulled up and set the emergency brake I got out to stretch. I envied a family I saw. The parents and children talked and laughed together. I saw three little girls with ponytails and sundresses. All I could do was pray for my child.

She had been gone for over 24 hours and who knew how Daniel was treating her? I couldn't let myself think of that. I had to keep my head. I took a deep breath of sea air and walked to the front of the ferry. As usual, the seagulls and dolphins were escorting us across. I remembered being a little girl and throwing bread to them. The sea air was so comforting and reminiscent of my childhood. I knew it would comfort me through the dark night ahead. I dreaded the quiet of the island when dark fell and all the happy young families had gone home.

When I got to the Port Aransas side I went straight to Buck's. Buck's was the water boat taxi that went to Carolina Key. I parked in the lot and went in. Willie, a slobbering basset hound, greeted me at the door. Willie had been at Buck's forever. I looked briefly around at the T shirts, flip flops, and seashells. I would need something to dig with and I selected a stout looking shovel. There were candy bars and sodas by the counter.

I paid for my ticket and shovel, then loaded my heavy sand bucket on the jetty boat. I covered the gold with a towel. I took a seat in the back and tried not to be conspicuous. Too few people would mean that I would stand out. I counted 12 others as we crowded together. This was a safe number. I tried to ignore everyone and not encourage conversation. I turned my face into the wind and pulled down the baseball cap I wore with sunglasses. Surely my modest Bermuda shorts and T shirt would not cause anyone to notice me. We departed as soon as we pulled up at the dock. It was the only manmade thing on the island except for the huge granite boulders that came from Marble Falls, TX.

I purposely lagged behind and let everyone pass me. I knew I had to find a place up in the vines to dig my hole. I walked a little ways inward and found a natural depression. As I crawled down into it I looked around to see how visible I would be. All around me the wind was blowing and the sun was shining. I counted six fishermen and about 20 beach combers. I looked at my watch. It was 2:30. I would have two hours to dig my hole. I had to get to work.

I spent a few minutes trying to pray as I sucked down a bottle of Gatorade. The hot sand did feel wonderful on my feet and I thought of all the times I had been here and the fun I had. I picked up my shovel and began digging. The hardest part was trying to keep the sides from caving in. It would take almost two hours and some achy muscles before I would have it stable enough.

Finally, the hole looked big enough and I tested it, laying down and moving my legs back and forth. The key to success was to cover my body but still be able to breathe. I picked a few vines to put over my face. The last thing I did before I got into my hole was go into the water and soak myself. The water felt wonderful and I struggled not to cry. I felt so alone. How could this be happening to my daughter? Why her? I knew that I could not afford to break down now. I prayed earnestly for strength, then squared my shoulders and clambered down inside the hole. I placed the sand bucket under a towel as a makeshift pillow. Then I lay down and fought a moment of claustrophobia. I pulled the sand in on top of me, first my feet, legs, and body. I gathered the sand up to my neck and covered my hair. I placed the vines over my face and then wiggled my arms until they were covered. Now for a long wait. I tried to sleep and eventually dozed off only to wake with a jerk when I heard the loud shout of a toddler. I could hear the sounds of people packing up and calling to one another. At any other time it would have been quite humorous.

"Lindy, I told you that fried chicken was going to be too rich for me. You know I get heartburn so easily these days," a man's voice said. I remembered this elderly man carrying his bag chair and newspaper.

"Well, Fred, no one told you to go eat five pieces of the durn stuff!" was his wife's sharp retort.

Slowly, their voices faded and I listened, not daring to move. More and more people passed by. I heard the boat coming across the harbor. Then silence. It was now 4:30 and I would have to sit tight until the security guard came by at 5:30. I tried to sleep but it would not come. I tried not to think of Grace and Philip. I tried to think of where the gold could have come from and how Daniel discovered it. What would he do when he found out we had hidden the gold from him? Would he just hand her over without a fight? Had he really killed Shirley? Was it possible it was someone else? If so, who? These questions swirled in my mind as I waited and waited.

Ch. 11
Sun. July 8, 2008
Philip

I looked at the screen of my phone and was dismayed to find Ken's number. "Hello, Ken?" I said.

"Hi, Philip. I was wondering how things are going?" he said.

"Just fine. I am out at the camp. I came to gather up Grace's belongings. How are things with you?" I asked.

"Well, I'm a little confused at the moment. I called out to the airport this morning and was told that there were not any flights to Memphis today nor were there any connecting flights to Memphis," he said and let the silence span between us. I sighed. I waited for a moment trying desperately to think of what to do.

"I'll be right over and I expect some straight answers," Ken said. The line went dead.

I picked up the can of Mountain Dew. I looked at it and shook it. I heard a rattle. I dumped the can out in my hand and was surprised to find a gum wrapper. I opened it up. "Candace" was written in Grace's handwriting. Ok? I thought. Who is Candace and what does this mean? It was obviously a clue from Grace. I had to smile. She loved to read mystery novels and watch Cold Case files on tv. She was actually thinking of working for the police department as a dispatcher. She had talked to Ken a couple of months ago and had volunteered at our local 911 center and a rape crisis center.

I was frustrated but there was nothing more I could do here. Not with Ken on his way. I walked back up the stairs to the dining room. Susan and another girl were sitting at a table eating ice cream. She looked surprised to see me.

"Mr. Stephens are you still here?" she asked.
"I am meeting Officer Ken here just to tie up a few loose ends. I was wondering, though, can you tell me who Candace is?"

"Oh sure. She works in the infirmary. Why?" she asked.

"Are she and Grace very close?" I asked.
"I don't think so," she answered, sharing a strange look with the other counselor.

"I just wondered. Well, I will see you girls later," I said and strode out of the building before having to answer any questions from overly curious young people. Well, that explained who Candace was. So, now someone else is involved, but why? Had Daniel taken Candace, too?

Ken was waiting for me by my truck in the parking lot. He took one look at my face and said simply, "Well?"

I stared at him for a long time, knowing I needed help but resisting from fear. A scripture, long ago memorized at my mother's knee popped into my mind. "For God gave us not a spirit of fearfulness; but of power and love and discipline." II Timothy 1:7.

"Daniel has Grace. Hope and I dug up the gold and she took it with her. She is hiding it in a safe place. I plan to meet her when I find Grace."

Ken looked at me for a long time. "And you couldn't tell me this? Come on, man. I am your brother in Christ. You kept this from me? Now Hope is out there all alone? Why didn't you want my help?" he sounded hurt.

"I was trying to be smart. He wants the gold. I felt like that was the only thing that I had that could keep Grace alive. I'm sorry." I sighed heavily, feeling the stress that had been building for hours now. Ken held out his hand. "Will you let me help you now?" he asked. I took his hand and shook it and nodded my head. "I'm just so confused. Why is all of this happening?" I asked.

"Let's go to your house. We need to talk and make some plans. I need to tell you what my investigators turned up on Daniel," he said.

The house was extremely quiet and I realized as I sank down at the dining table that I had never had lunch. We called for a delivered pizza and Ken called his wife to tell her he would meet her at the prayer service. She said that one of their twin boys had come down with a cold and she would not be able to make it.

"When one comes down with it they all will take it within the week," Ken joked. He and his wife Linda had four and eight year old boys and the twins were one. He waited until I had eaten and then he began to explain what his team had discovered about Daniel. He laid a thick envelope on the table between us. "It's not good. Apparently he has been leading a double life. He was born in Waco to Stacy Johnson in 1990, father unknown. She was only 16 at the time. She married Ray Joseph when Daniel was four and he was placed in a foster home for the first time later that year. He lived in foster homes off and on until he was eight. Parental rights were revoked and he was adopted by the Fergusons. Ray Joseph is now in jail for a burglary gone wrong that bought him 10 years in federal prison. No one knows what happened to Stacy Johnson. She became homeless after Daniel was adopted and no one has heard from her since. It's possible that they have had some contact but very unlikely." He looked up at me then and took off his glasses. "He's been in a gang. He has some ties to the Vietnamese Mafia. There was a gang in his old neighborhood. He's never served any time, except for one or two juvenile offences. The camp was aware of these but took him on anyway on the condition that his gang activity ceased. For all intents and purposes, since high school he has kept his nose clean."

"Ken, I'm sorry, I don't know what to tell you. Last night, we were scared, we weren't thinking clearly, we didn't have much time to plan. We were going on gut instinct and that was to ensure Grace's safety the only way we knew how. It's 5:45. I promised Lance I would be at the prayer service. He needs all the support he can get. Can we go now and try to formulate a plan when we return?" I asked.

"Yes, of course. I just want you to know that I am here for you as long as it takes to bring your family back together," Ken said.

We left then and went to what was a very heartfelt service with many tears, lots of hugs and a tremendous outpouring of affection for Lance and his family. We returned about 7:30 and began to plan a strategy. I had filled Ken in on all of the phone calls we had received. The cell number was always different each time he called.

"That tells me he is around other people, in a public location. It also means that Grace's chances of escaping are good. Since you have spoken to her it suggests that he is not leaving her on her own. What we need to do now is find out more about these coins.

Where is Hope? How are you contacting her?" Ken asked.

"She went down to Port Aransas. She is burying the gold on Carolina Key. We have not had any contact since she left. The island doesn't have any satellite connection. She was spending the night there. I'm sure she will call me in the morning from Corpus Christi. I told her to stop there and get cash and supplies. Our plan was to hide out in Hot Springs, Arkansas. We have been there several times on vacation and she is familiar with the area. I didn't want her driving by herself somewhere she didn't know, so that's why we picked Hot Springs," I said.

"That's actually a very good plan. However, I don't want her to contact you directly after she gets settled in Hot Springs. It's too dangerous," Ken warned.

"You must find some alternative to a cell phone or land line. It's too easily traced," he said.
We spoke for an hour or so after that making plans and wondering how this had all happened and wondering where to go from here. Ken left about 10:00 to get home to his family. He left me with a handshake and a prayer, confirming his commitment to stand by Hope and I until we got Grace back. He was a great comfort to me that night.

Ch. 12
5:00 p.m. Carolina Key
Sun. July 8, 2008
Hope

The heat made me feel drowsy and I slept off and
on for the next hour or so. I longed to look
at my watch but I knew that it would be safer to
remain hidden. I awoke with a start when I
heard the low rumble of the security guard's 4
wheeler. I was suddenly filled with fear. What if
I were caught? How would I ever get Grace back?
How different my emotions were now as opposed to
when I was here as a carefree, young teenager. We
had fought to keep our nervous giggles quiet.

   I caught sight of the security guard out of the
corner of my eye as he passed by, sand flying
out behind his wheels. He wore a florescent safety
vest and a tan beach hat. He drove about half
way down the beach and made a big u turn and
headed back to the dock. Not too concerned
about stowaways, I guess. I felt much better when I
heard him slam the gate to the dock and lock it. I
wiggled my legs a little bit to ease their cramping and
longed to get up. I didn't dare.   There was still a
good three to four hours of daylight left, but I could
at least wiggle.

   My arms were stiff and my feet had pins and
needles. I fought another wave of claustrophobia so I
removed the vines from my face.

   Ah, I could breathe in some much needed fresh air.
That helped. I tried to gather my thoughts. Surely I
could think of some way to be productive in all this
mess. I prayed for Philip. I wondered how he had
spent his day. I prayed for Lance. He was going to

be so lost without Shirley.

The hours until sunset passed slowly. I finally felt safe enough to uncover myself and creep in the darkness into the water to relieve myself. That Gatorade was good for keeping me hydrated but not good for my tiny bladder. I listened for boats. They would be the danger until morning. I uncovered my sandwich which had been mashed flat by me laying on it. For the first time in two days I was actually hungry. I wondered if Daniel was feeding Grace properly. I wondered if he had mistreated her. I prayed for her safety.

I knew I needed to rest but about midnight I could bear my restless heart no more and I ventured out for a walk. The waves crashing on the shore were soothing as was the quiet. Somehow I could make it until morning. There was little to do but wait. I slept fitfully, and when I did awake in the early morning hours, my eyes felt glued together. The sand and wind had made them sticky, red, and irritated. I couldn't wait to wash my face in fresh, cold water. The wind was up and had a damp chill to it.

The tricky part of my reemergence in society would be when the early beach combers came on the 8:00 boat. I knew they would head immediately down the beach as fast as possible. They would grab every sand dollar and star fish that had washed up overnight. I couldn't afford to have any footprints seen on the shore. The overnight waves had washed away my footprints from my midnight walk.

I would have to time it just right. I couldn't let anyone realize I wasn't on the first boat. I

wondered about my car and if anyone had noticed it
in the parking lot. There were usually plenty of cars
parked overnight in that lot. I decided to stay put
until the 8:30 boat arrived and I could try to blend in
with them.

I needed some way of marking the hiding place
for the gold, something that would not be washed
away with the tide. The 8:00 a.m. boat was packed
with 2 families of 5 and 7 senior citizens. This made
me feel better. I would have no trouble blending in.
The 8:30 boat was full as well and as soon as the first
wave of beach combers passed me I began to wiggle
out of my confining hole. I tried to sit up casually
and uncover my legs and feet. I had to sit for several
minutes because my calves were asleep. Gradually
the feeling came back and I was able to get up.

I arranged the sand bucket upside down over the
gold and prayed for a moment thinking of Shirley.
She had died because of Daniel's greed for wealth. I
thought of the scripture in Matthew 6:19, "Lay not up
for yourselves treasures on earth where moth and rust
doth corrupt, and thieves break through and steal."
What a waste her death was! She was my friend and I
would miss her greatly.

Sadly, I pushed the sand back over the hole and
packed it down. I walked down the hill to the beach.
Two women were walking towards me carrying
bright colored bags over their shoulders. I bent over
and searched for sand dollars.

"Good morning." they greeted me. "Having any
luck?" one asked. I nodded and smiled, but
kept quiet and turned away as soon as possible and
walked into the water. It was freezing cold
but I was desperate to relieve my bladder. I took a

deep breath and plunged under the surf. When I came up my first thought was of Grace. Oh, if only I could swim to her right now.

I walked over to the dock and counted my paces to the hole. Straight from the dock it was 80 paces and left inland 50 paces. I would have to write this down as soon as I got to the car or I would never remember it. A sobering thought came to me. I should call Philip and let him know the coordinates in case something happened to me.

I got on the 9:00 boat back to Buck's and eavesdropped on two women who were from Austin. No one seemed to notice that I hadn't been on an earlier boat. I ducked my head when I passed the captain of our little boat but he merely raised his coffee cup to his mouth and waved me aboard. I was relieved to have pulled it off. I was also very sleepy and hungry and ready for a cup of coffee.

It had only taken me a few minutes to bury the sand bucket filled with gold coins. I wondered what someone would think if their children dug it up? They would be shocked, of course. If it stayed undiscovered then we could always come back and get it once we had Grace back. For now, like Philip said, hiding the gold was the only way to ensure her safety.   Right now I had only one goal and that was to get myself together and get some breakfast and coffee. Then I would drive to Corpus Christi and stock up on supplies and get cash. I couldn't wait to get to my phone to call Philip.

Back safely at Buck's with no one the wiser that I had stowed away all night, I was greeted by Willie. I gave him a pat and then made a bee line for the McDonald's next door. I availed myself of their wonderful air conditioned bathroom and then slurped down a large latte. My hands still shook in fear every time I thought about Grace but I knew I needed to get through this. I was hungry and I forced down some breakfast noticing even at a time like this how comforting a McDonald's can smell.

The first thing I did when I reached my car was to charge my phone and check my voice mail for messages.   The drive to Corpus Christi was uneventful and the traffic was light. I was halfway there when my phone rang. I didn't recognize the number and my heart began to pound as I quickly pulled to the shoulder. I didn't trust myself to continue driving. I wanted to focus completely on this call. It was indeed, Daniel. He was very unhappy.

"Mrs. Stephens, this is Daniel. I thought you understood the plan. Do you not value your daughter's life? I thought you did. Was I wrong?" he asked.

"No, no Daniel. I want to cooperate and I don't want Grace harmed but I know that if I give you the gold Grace may not have a chance. Please, please give her back to us. Please!" I struggled not to cry.

"I'm warning you, I've waited years to get to that gold. I need it! You'd better talk to your husband and get him to bring me the coins. Once he does, then I will decide what to do with Grace." abruptly, the line went dead. I held the phone for several moments before I realized that this time he had not let me talk to Grace. I pulled into a roadside park to call Philip. He answered on the first ring. "Hi, honey," I said.

"Hope, are you ok?" he asked.
"Yes, I'm fine. Everything worked out ok. No one saw me, at least as far as I could tell and I am halfway to Corpus. I just spoke with Daniel. He called on my cell. I didn't even know he had this number," I said.

"Well, I'm sure he got it from Grace. Did you talk to her?" he asked. "No, and that really scared me. He wants you to bring him the coins, now. He also said something weird. He said he had waited years to get to the gold. Wonder what that means?" I asked.
"I don't know, but I need to let you know we have some help. Ken was here last night and he is committed to helping us through this. He called the airport and found out there were not any flights to Memphis. He is the only one who knows. Last night we went to a prayer service for Shirley. It was great support for Lance. He is having a really hard time. Ken wants to get you safely to Hot Springs but he doesn't want you to contact me using the cell or land line after you arrive. We have to come up with an alternative way to communicate," Philip said.

"You know Philip, I've been thinking, how much is this gold worth anyway?" I asked.

"I don't know. I wouldn't think it would be worth that much in this market but Daniel may not have any idea what it is worth. He's a former gang member and a kid that was passed around from parent to foster care. He may just be imagining a fortune. He said he wants the coins and then he would decide what to do with Grace. He hung up before I could ask to talk to her," I said. The line was silent for a moment and I knew he was thinking of the potential dangers Grace was facing all alone.

"Did you make me a reservation at K.O.A.? It will be night before I get there," I said.

"Not yet, but I will. I want to talk to Ken as soon as he gets here, about this latest contact and then I will call you about lunch time, ok?" he asked.

"Ok, I love you," I said.

"I love you, too. Keep strong and keep praying. Philipians 4:13, remember?" he said.

"I remember."

I found the Walmart in Corpus and stopped to buy my supplies, get cash, and get gas. It was about four hours later when I received another call from Philip. I had begun to get hungry and had stopped for lunch and to stretch my legs. Emotionally, I was doing pretty good.

"Hello?" I said.

"Hi, babe. It's me. How are you doing?" Philip asked.

"I'm doing ok. Any news?" I asked.

"Nothing about Grace. Where are you?" he asked.

"I am almost to the state line," I answered.

"You are making good time. I called the KOA and got you a reservation. The people there are as nice as usual. I asked them to put you close to the bathhouse under a light because you were traveling alone. They have installed a security guard that patrols all night. Remember the big homeless population they have on Bathhouse Row?" he asked.

"Yes, I remember that guy that asked us for food," I answered.

"Well, anyway, Ken has found some interesting facts. Lance called me this morning and said he was cleaning out his spare room for the kids to stay a few days and came across some of the papers of Shirley's Dad's that she went through the night before she died," he said.

"Yes, I remember her saying she was going to," I interrupted.

"Well, Lance found a safe deposit box key," Philip said.

"A safe deposit box key? What's in it?" I asked.

"Lance doesn't know. He was going to contact Shirley's sister and ask her. Ken says that because of the murder if he needs to he can secure a court order to open it," Philip said.

"Well, that's odd. Maybe it's just some old love letters, or something."

"Sure, or it could be something regarding the camp or their house," Philip responded.

"I'll call you back when I know more. How are you holding up?" he asked, ever thoughtful.

"Well, I would much rather be at home with you and Grace. I am doing as well as I can on only a few hours sleep. It has been a long time since I pulled an all-nighter." I laughed.

"I'm sorry. I know it was hard for you to spend the night alone and everything. It's going to be ok. We are going to get her back. There are so many scriptures going through my mind right now and I want to share them with you. First though, we need to make a plan for contacting each other when you reach Hot Springs. At this point, we can't know who else at the camp may be involved so Ken doesn't want you to call here. When I was at the camp yesterday I was in one of the older storage buildings and I saw a telex machine in pretty good shape. Do you think you can remember how to use one if you could possibly find one?" he asked.

"Are you crazy?" I laughed. "That's how you proposed to me. Of course, I remember how to use one."

"Ok, I will let you go now and try to gather some more information. I will call you if I hear from Grace or Daniel and please be careful driving." Philip said.

"I will. I love you. We'll be together soon.

"Bye," I said feeling a lump in my throat.

After several more hours driving I entered Arkansas, then Hot Springs. The drive was beautiful as usual. Arkansas was one of my favorite states and I particularly favored Northern Arkansas around Lake Catherine. Late summer was too soon for the autumn leaves to change, but when they did the color was spectacular. It was late when I pulled into the campground and I was tired but I was also hungry and feeling very lonely. I wanted desperately to talk to Aunt Ruth, just to hear her voice, assuring me that everything was going to be ok, but I didn't trust myself emotionally. My nerves were too frazzled and I was feeling too vulnerable.

When I checked in I ordered a pizza and I sat on the porch swing of my little cabin and ate. By the time I finished, it was dark. I went inside and lay down on the bed. I reached for my cell phone and saw I missed a call from Philip. I called him back and Ken answered. He said Philip was taking a shower and I spent about 30 minutes talking to him about Daniel's background, Shirley's death, and the plans for her funeral.

"Hope, Philip just walked in. I will let you two talk and we will contact you tomorrow sometime. I've got to go relieve Linda, now all the boys are sick!" Ken said.

"Hi, babe. How are you doing?" Philip said.

"Good," I answered. We spoke for a few minutes before I asked if there was any new information regarding Grace or Daniel.

"We have not been able to track down Daniel's mother Stacy. I found a Mountain Dew can in the closet of the infirmary with Grace's ring in it and a gum wrapper with the name Candace. We are trying to track down the whereabouts of Candace and her daughter," Philip said.

"Candace? From the camp infirmary? You think she could be involved in this?" I asked, shocked.

"It's always a possibility," he said.

"Lance spoke to Shirley's sister, Rebecca, and she knew nothing about a safe deposit box. Richard has only been gone just over a year, I don't think they have really looked his papers over. Rebecca lives in Washington, you know," Philip said.

"No, I didn't know that," I said.

"Lance is going to open the box tomorrow. Rebecca faxed over a consent form today. Maybe whatever is in there will give us some new information."

"It seems doubtful to me," I answered.
"Babe, I love you. Have faith," he said.
We prayed together and then hung up. I was sure to put my phone on charge before going to bed. I visited the bathhouse for a much needed shower, rinsing off the grunge of sand and grit.

Ch. 13
Tues. July 10, 2008
Phillip

        The alarm went off and I stumbled into the shower, realizing that this was the 3rd day without my daughter at home. I prayed for her and for Lance as I laid out a clean suit for the funeral. John had called last night and asked me to lead the congregation in singing. I managed to eat a couple of pieces of toast and drink some coffee. I was rinsing my dishes when the phone rang. My heart skipped a beat, thinking of Grace and Hope. My hand shook on the receiver. "Hello?" I said.

        "Philip? It's Auntie," Aunt Ruth said.
"Hello, Auntie. How are you today?" I asked.

        "Doing fine. How are my girls?" Ruth asked. "They are ok, they are visiting with my folks. I am just heading out to a funeral. The owner of the camp where Grace has been working was killed by an intruder. They are members of our church and her husband is pretty broken up about it," I said.

        There was a very long silence. "Ruth? Are you there?" I asked, thinking we were cut off. I wondered if Daniel had somehow tampered with my phone.

        "Philip, are you talking about Richard Watson's daughter?" Ruth asked in a strange voice.
"Yes, did you know them?" I asked.

        "Yes... well, I knew of them," she replied.
"Well, the service starts soon, so I need to run but I will tell Hope you called when I talk to her," I said.

"You do that, dear. Take care," Ruth said, and hung up.

The funeral was being held in the dining hall of the camp. It was big enough to accommodate friends, family, and the members of our church in town, Mountain Creek Church of Christ. I got there early and placed a song booklet on each chair. Shirley's family had requested all the old funeral favorites like, "Precious Memories, Farther Along, and When We All Get to Heaven."

.   Soon the workers from the funeral home came and brought Shirley's casket and many flowers from well wishers. I saw the children before the service and gave them all a tearful hug. I told them that Hope sent her love and was sorry she couldn't be here for them.

The service opened with a prayer and then I began the singing. Her son read the 121 Psalm and another relative gave her eulogy. Our minister, Roger Edwards, gave a short sermon about the joys awaiting us in heaven, and encouraging us to forgive the person who had purposely cut short the life of a woman so many loved. There were many tears from the audience. Lance had asked me to sit with the family and I kept a protective hand on his back as he wept. His children were a comfort to him and I was glad that they were all here.

At the close of the service, there was a photo slideshow of Shirley, her family, and the camp. It was set to a beautiful hymn, and it was very emotional to see the faces of the many children Shirley had helped. Suddenly, the screen went black. For a moment, no one reacted. We all assumed it was a technical problem. Then, a live video feed of Grace filled the screen, and I stood up in surprise. She was sitting in a chair and had her hands tied behind her and her feet were tied to the chair.

" Daddy?" she said in a shaking voice.

My mouth was so dry I almost couldn't speak.

"I'm here, Grace. I love you," I said, wondering if this would be the last time I would see my beautiful girl alive.

"I love you, too," she said, sobbing.

"Daddy, Daniel said if you don't bring the gold coins to Mountain Creek under the big willow tree at 2a.m. tonight, he will kill me," she said.

I could tell she was trying to be brave. The video panned to Daniel who held a knife, I am assuming the one that killed Shirley, against Grace's throat. Grace closed her eyes and I felt my stomach churn. For a moment, I thought I would pass out.

"You've been warned," Daniel said, and the screen went black. There was a loud murmuring from the audience as everyone began to talk at once. Ken took charge and instructed everyone to remain calm. He requested that Brother Edwards end the service with a prayer, both for Shirley's family and Grace's safety. As soon as Brother Edwards finished, Ken came to me and escorted me to my car.

When we got home Ken and I sat for a couple of hours discussing the possibilities of capturing Daniel and how we would handle the drop tonight. I was just exhausted from the day and all the sleepless nights I had endured. Ken was very helpful fielding phone calls from Lance, John, Bette, and other members of the church family. I thought about lying down on the sofa for a while but I knew I should call Hope and fill her in.

Ch. 14
Tues. July 10, 2008
Hope

I slept fitfully and awakened to the sound of ducks quacking softly. I smiled for the first time in days. The ducks I remembered from our travels when Grace was younger. They always woke us up quacking. The KOA has a pancake breakfast and coffee served every morning. I went to the little café and got myself a large coffee and pancake to go. I ate on my porch swing and fed the ducks my scraps. I returned to my porch and sat watching the other campers loading into vans and SUVs for a day of sightseeing. I wondered where they were going.

Bathhouse Row was very famous. The Mid America Science Museum was popular. I saw an advertisement for an exhibit on the human body. On an ordinary trip that might be interesting. Today, however all I wanted was a phone call telling me my daughter was safe and I could go home. Sighing, I went inside my small cabin to take stock of what I had and what I would need to buy if I was going to be here several days. I made a list and headed out to Walmart. They were stocking lunch boxes and school supplies. I remembered Grace's favorite lunch box was the Mystery Machine from Scooby Doo.

I moved slowly up and down the aisles in a fog trying to imagine staying here alone for maybe a week. What would I possibly do with myself? Maybe I could get a job, just temporarily, anything to keep my mind off of things. I would consider it and talk to Phillip tonight. I had to do something more to help Grace than just sitting around.

I left Walmart and cruised around, familiarizing myself with the downtown area. The Hot Springs Park was beautiful and crowded with summer tourists. Bathhouse Row was the main street. Philip and I had taken a tour of the Ford House once. Quapaw Bathhouse was further down. I felt too restless to go back to the campground, so I went to see the Human Body Exhibit I saw advertised at the Mid America Science Museum. When Grace was younger she loved the robotic dinosaur exhibit.

I bought a ticket and strolled around slowly, knowing Phillip was not scheduled to call until after the funeral. I couldn't believe Shirley was to be buried today and I wasn't even there to bid my friend a farewell or to show my love to her children and husband. I prayed for her family and mine every few minutes. I comforted myself with the thought that one day we would be together in glory and I would again be able to praise the Lord with her. Entering the museum store, I noticed a Help Wanted sign in the snack bar. There was a woman about my age waiting on a long line of customers. I gave her a smile as I examined science kits and books that Grace would have enjoyed when she was younger. When the line went down I ordered some lunch and chatted with the attendant. Her name was Rosa.

When I inquired about the job, she encouraged me to apply even if it was only temporary. I explained to her that I had kitchen experience cooking for 100. She told me if I was interested to come back tomorrow and speak to the manager. I drove back to the downtown area, restless and looking for something to distract myself. I pulled into a parking place on Bathhouse Row and began to walk. When I reached the Ford Bathhouse I went in just for something to do. The woman at the desk must have been bored herself because she chatted happily with me for a long time and then led me on a private tour.

Her name was Janice. She told me about all the old celebrities that used the bathhouse. She also told me about her grandchildren. She was very kind and I enjoyed myself very much.

As we were nearing the end of the tour, we entered a small room that Janice described as an office. It contained a beautiful roll top desk, a brass coat rack, and an antique typewriter. On a table in the corner I was amazed to see a telex machine on a stand. I almost gasped but I caught myself just in time. Casually, I inquired about it and she told me the telex was still in working order and had been donated by a charity organization who wanted it out of their storage unit.

"I guess there are a lot of these old machines around in someone's garage or basement." Janice said. I thanked her for the tour and told her I might be back sometime that week. She seemed excited, and bid me farewell. I could barely restrain myself from running back to the car. When I reached it, I jumped in and drove with haste to the campground and called Philip. Disappointed, I talked to the answering machine briefly, just asking him to call me back. I used the small workout room at the campground to burn off some energy. I was missing Grace and Philip badly and I needed something constructive to do. It seemed like hours until Philip called. I was trying to concentrate on a novel when my phone rang. I snatched it open and said hello. Phillip's voice quavered when he told me about Shirley's funeral and the Skype video of Grace.

"Don't worry honey, she's alive and apparently well for the moment. She looked like she was trying to be brave and I know she is persevering. She has strength. She's going to make it through this," he said. I could hear the fear in his voice and hot tears rolled down my cheeks.

"How can you be so certain? Why is this happening to us?" I cried into the phone and I felt terrible for doing it because I knew it would make Phillip feel bad. He sounded so weary. I just couldn't help the feeling of despair that was falling around me.

"Ken is going to coordinate all the surveillence and we are going to make the drop tonight at 2 a.m. We expect to apprehend Daniel tonight. He'll never make it out of the park. I promise honey. I will have Grace back tonight and we will come get you. Maybe make a vacation of it," he said.

"I wish I could believe that," I said.

"Pray for me. I need to go, Ken needs to make some calls and the doorbell is ringing," Phillip said.

"Call me as soon as you have her! I love you both so much. I'll be praying the whole time," I said. As I hung up I dropped to my knees to pray by the bed. Surely this time the Lord will answer my prayers and I would have my daughter home.

Ch. 15
Tues. July 10, 2008
Aunt Ruth

Ruth stepped inside the doorway and looked around. She was tiny and pretty and I wondered if she had lived if this is what Carol, Hope's mom, would have looked like. She had been gone for 20 years now. I had never met her but Ruth meant everything to Hope.

Ruth looked steadily at Ken and asked me bluntly, "Can he be trusted?"

Ken gave me an incredulous look, then proceeded to introduce himself as a family friend, a member of law enforcement and to reassure her that he was more than trustworthy. She looked up at him and nodded, giving her approval. "I knew your mother," she said, as if that settled everything.

"Put on some coffee." she instructed Ken. I tried not to laugh as he moved around my kitchen, asking her if she took cream and sugar. When we were settled with our coffee at the table, Ruth asked us not to ask any questions until she was through.

"When you called me to tell me that Grace was missing I knew that it had all come back," she said.

"What? What do you know?" I began to sputter.

She held up a tiny hand. I tried to control myself but I was feeling so frustrated with a lack of information I wanted to scream. I took a deep breath and she placed her hands on mine.

"Perhaps we should pray," she said.

We each bowed our heads silently for a few moments and when I lifted my head I saw the peace on her face. I wasn't sure mine reflected the same peace but I did feel calmer. She took a deep breath and began, "Richard Watson was a missionary in Vietnam. Norman was stationed there as well. They met and became good friends. It was a small town called Da Nang. There was an orphanage that Richard worked with. All the orphanages there are run by nuns. Richard tried very hard to get medical supplies and food to them as well as bibles. One day a man came to Richard. He had the gold coins. He gave them to Richard with a check and said he had heard about the orphanage and he wanted to help. Richard didn't like having that much gold around but he didn't ask any questions. He assumed the gold came from a less than desirable source but he was determined to put that money to good use.

Norman was being transferred back to the states and Richard gave the money and coins to him to convert into U.S. dollars. He shipped out within 2 days to Frankfurt, Germany. Two weeks later, two members of the Vietnamese mafia broke into the mission and demanded the coins back. They left Richard with two broken legs and forced him to give them Norman's name and address. At the army post in Germany Norman set up an offshore account for Richard. He put the money in the missions name and flew home. He and Carol were on their way to see me for the first time in several years. They had moved around so much in the service. When Hope was young and Norman was away on assignment Carol and Hope would come and stay with me. During the war, however, when Norman wasn't on tour in Vietnam, they were stationed in Germany."

"What happened to Richard?" asked Ken, getting impatient.

"He spent two weeks in the hospital with a concussion recovering. Incidently, the man who donated the coins to Richard was found floating in a rice patty with a bullet in his back."

"The mafia doesn't play very nice." Ken said.

"No, I'm afraid they don't."

"So, after they got to Port Aransas?" I asked.

She looked at me sadly and then I knew.

"They never arrived in Port Aransas. I received a call around midnight. I had been waiting for them for hours by then. I made it to the hospital in time to see Carol. Norman was already dead. I think Carol held on long enough to see me to make sure that I would care for Hope. Hope was 18 and doing fine in college. She knew I would take care of her, but I guess as a mother she needed to hear the words. She told me the men had followed them for miles before running them off the road and over an embankment. The car rolled over several times. She told me the money was waiting for Richard in an offshore account," Ruth said.

"What about the gold coins that Hope found?" I asked.

"During the war they were able to convert the check into cash for the account but they were not able to convert the coins. During the war they just didn't have the resources. Carol told me that Norman had shipped the coins to me in a piece of furniture," she said.

Ken and I stared at each other. "A table?" we asked together.

"Yes, a table with a glass top," she replied. We looked at each other with disbelief. I ran my hands through my hair. This was too much to deal with.

"What happened to the offshore account?" Ken asked.

Ruth smiled and got up from the table. She stretched and took a deep breath. She stood looking out the window.

"The money was put to good use. It went to help children," she said. She turned around and looked at us steadily. She put her hands on the table and leaned down.

"The money provided for the purchase of Indian Oaks Christian Camp," she said and smiled.

Ken's mouth dropped open and I'm sure my face registered my own surprise.
"So... how did you know Richard and Vanessa, Shirley's Mom and Dad?" I asked.

"Vanessa grew up here in Mountain Creek. Her family was from here. When Richard came back from Vietnam they settled down here and purchased the camp. I met them when I brought them the table. Ken, that's also when I met your mother. She was working in the kitchen with Vanessa doing the job that Hope has been doing until Grace went missing. Richard, Vanessa, and I discussed it and we knew we must keep Hope and Shirley safe. The mafia didn't have any other contacts without Richard and Norman.   Richard's mission was very careful to keep any information about his condition at the hospital under wraps. The nuns put out a story that he died from his injuries," Ruth said.
"They lied?" I asked. Ken and Ruth both gave me a disgusted look.

"So, Richard and Vanessa ended up with the gold coins. Shirley inherited the table, which she put in the apartment Daniel was staying in. He found them. Somehow he discovered they were real and put them in a lockbox which someone opened and Hope found." Ken said.

"Then Shirley buried them, Hope and I dug them up and Hope has now reburied them on Carolina Key," I said, shaking my head. "Man!"
"Did Shirley ever know any of this?" asked Ken.

"I would think not," Ruth replied. "She and Lance had just married and their children were small, Rebecca was still in high school. They were only told that Richard was injured during a robbery at the mission." Ruth said.

We all jumped as the phone rang. Thinking it was Hope, I was wondering how I was going to tell her everything as I answered the phone. It was Officer Hodge, calling to say that everything was set and ready for the meeting. I will have a duffle bag ready with coins weighing approximately 32 lbs. There will be officers waiting in the parking lot to check for cars coming and going.

The next few hours were tense as we waited, sometimes dreading the moment and sometimes anxiously anticipating it. It would come soon enough. Ruth did not wait around for anything. She immediately took over the kitchen and soon had bread baking. She telephoned Hope and spent an hour praying with her, reassuring her, and explaining the facts surrounding her parents death.

We ate a late dinner and I lay down in my room for a couple of hours. Ken went home to see his family and Ruth sat up in the living room, crocheting and praying. She said it helped her to stay calm. I spoke to Hope and though she was having a hard time believing what had happened to her folks and was still worried about Grace, she was doing ok.

Ken and Hodge came to get me at midnight and brought the duffle bag and a bullet proof vest for me to wear. Ruth joined us in prayer before we left and I knew whatever happened that she would be here for Grace and Hope.

"Bring them home, Phillip," Ruth said as the door closed behind me.

Ch. 16
2:00 a.m. Wed.
July 11, 2008
Phillip

I stood under the canopy of the willow tree in the pitch dark. There was no moon, only a heavy dew and light mist coming up from the water. I had a flashlight, a powerful one, Ken had given me that many of the officers carried more for protection than lighting. In the back of my mind I saw the sharp knife held against my daughter's throat. My heart sank and I felt sick whenever I remembered her tears. I could feel anger building inside me and I wanted to shout to Daniel that he was a weak coward, preying on women and children. In the silence, I wondered if keeping me waiting was just a sick joke or if he was looking for the police presence he had to know was here. I checked my cell. 2:15 a.m. At 2:30, I heard the rumble of a 4 wheeler. I could hear it coming closer and closer but I couldn't see it. I began to stumble backwards and for a moment I almost panicked. It was going to run right over me. Suddenly, a bright light shone in my face.

"Drop it! Drop it right there!" Daniel screamed. I was so startled I dropped the duffle bag to the ground and stepped back. Daniel gunned the ATV forward and picked up the duffle. I could just make out a female figure on the back of the 4 wheeler. My heart leapt!
"Grace! Grace!" I yelled. Dousing the light and plunging me back into total darkness, Daniel gunned the engine.
"No, wait!" I screamed, running blindly in circles trying desperately to catch up.

"Wait!" I sobbed.

I ran as fast as I could, fists clenched, vowing in my heart to kill Daniel when I caught him. It was an evil thought but all I could think of was looking my wife in the eye and telling her I hadn't gotten Grace back. I heard a thump and a muffled cry. Closer to the street I could make out a figure on the ground. Daniel had thrown Grace off the 4 wheeler. I ran to her. I knelt and took her into my arms. Her mouth was taped shut and a gray hoodie covered her face. She was crying, her voice hoarse and she was making sounds trying to talk through the tape. Her hands were bound together and duct tape even covered her eyes.

"It's okay, baby. Daddy's here, Grace. I've got you now. It's all over." I said trying to comfort her. The relief I felt was overwhelming. She continued to squirm and cry even louder. I couldn't understand it. Was she hurt? Did she break something when she fell? I barely had time to think before Ken came rushing up to us.

"Is she hurt?" he asked. I winced as I looked into the turning light of the patrol car. He pulled a knife from his pocket and cut the tape on Grace's wrists. She was thrashing about on the ground, moaning loudly.

"Grace, hold still. I'm trying to cut you lose," Ken said.

"Honey, this might hurt. I'm going to pull the tape off your eyes. I'll try to be careful," he said.

He pulled the tape off her eyes and I ripped the tape from her mouth as she reached up to uncover her hoodie. I gasped as her short, white blond hair was revealed.

"Mr. Stephens, I'm so sorry. I tried to stop him." It was Candace. I stared at her for a long time, then turned away as the tears came. I leaned against the patrol car and sobbed. I felt so lost and empty. What could I possibly say to Hope now after I had convinced her to do the unthinkable and run off and hide the gold? Could she ever forgive me?

I covered my eyes with my hands like a child. Ken put his arms around me.

"Is she dead? Ken, is she dead?" I clutched at his shirt front.

"No, no man. She's not dead. Candace said he's taken Grace with him and her daughter Charlie. He's got two hostages now," Ken said. He turned away to answer a call held out to him by one of the many officers swarming around us.

Later in the hospital after Ken interrogates her, Candace asks to speak to Phillip and Hodge brings him to the hospital.

"Mr. Stephens, I know I have no right to ask you this but I'm begging you to forgive me. I swear I didn't know what I was getting into. I've made so many mistakes in my life and right now my daughter is paying for them. I thank God that Grace is with Charlie." She paused to take a breath, tears rolling down her cheeks. She was in obvious pain from three broken ribs. She looked much too young to be a mother and I felt compassion for her stirring in my soul.

"I promise you Grace hasn't been hurt. I didn't mean to find the gold. I didn't know what to do with it. Daniel has never had anything and I think all those years of being on the outside did something to him. He wants to be good but he doesn't know how. I met Shirley when I was 13. I had my grandmother with me until I was 15. After she died I kind of lost my way. That's when I got into trouble and got mixed up with Daniel. I got pregnant and I knew I had to make my life something better for her like Granny did for me. Shirley showed me how.

"Do you have any idea where he could be keeping Grace?" I asked.

"His mom has a house in Waco. It's being paid for by some Chinese guy." Candace replied.

"That's all I know. I only helped him because he threatened to take Charlie away from me and tell everyone that she is his. It turns out he took her anyway, but he promised to get her back to me. Right now I have to believe that she's going to be ok and God is watching over her. I have to keep on having faith," Candace said, putting her hand on mine.

"Yes, we both must keep our faith." I smiled at her. "Do you mind if I pray for us?" I asked.

Tears came to her eyes as she nodded her head and reached for my hand. As I prayed for Grace and Charlie, it came to me that I knew someone who would greatly benefit this young lady.

On my way out of the hospital, I spoke with Candace's doctor who agreed to release her at noon, into Aunt Ruth's capable hands.

Ch. 17
Wed. evening
July 11, 2008
Phillip

Phillip opened the door and called out, "Ruth, I'm home." Ruth came from the kitchen wearing an apron of Hope's that said, "Indian Oaks". The house smelled heavenly of fresh oranges, cinnamon and yeast bread.

"I have someone here I would like you to meet. This is Candace Bradshaw. Her daughter Charlie is now with Grace. I want you to take her under your wing." Candace looked shyly at Ruth, as if she were afraid of being rejected. Ruth, noticing her hesitation, took Candace's hand between both of her own and patted it.

"Come with me, my dear. I think we are going to be very good friends. We are both missing someone precious to us. I have made some of my famous cinnamon rolls. Would you like some tea?"

Phillip shook his head affectionately and started up the stairs for a shower and a nap. When he came down in the late afternoon he found the guest room made up for Candace and the two ladies setting the table for dinner. A savory smell permeated the kitchen and Phillip grinned.

"Chicken pot pie?" he asked Ruth.

"As soon as you ask the blessing," she replied, indicating his chair at the head of the table. The three of them got settled at the table and joined hands. For a long moment after they bowed their heads, Phillip tried to compose his emotions.

"Father God, we come to you in faith, in hope, and in love. You know that Grace and Charlie are still away from us, and we want to pray for their safety and well being. Help us to have the strength to forgive Daniel for what he has taken from us." Phillip's voice faltered and Ruth squeezed his hand.

"Thank you for letting us be together tonight. Thank you for this meal and bless the hands that prepared it. In Jesus' name, Amen."

Phillip coughed and cleared his throat. During the meal they relaxed together and enjoyed the fellowship. Shortly after they finished their coffee and dessert of cinnamon rolls, the doorbell rang.

"Wonder who that could be?" Phillip asked as he got up from his chair and opened the door. The anxious look on his face betrayed his frayed emotions. Clearly, he was hoping against hope that it would be his family returning to him.

"Lance, come in, come in. How are you doing? Do you need anything?" Phillip's concern was evident in his face and his voice. Ruth got up silently and went for the coffee pot.

"I just came from opening the safety deposit box and I found something unusual. Officer Ken was with me and he said I should bring this over immediately."

"What is it?" Philip asked.

"It's a photo," he said, handing it over. Phillip took the photo and stared at an image of a man's forearm with a large dragon tattoo. He placed it in the center of the table with a card that read, "Watch for the son."

"Watch for the son?" Candace read. "Does that mean something? Tong has a tattoo like that."

The hair stood up on the back of Phillip's neck and his eyes narrowed suspiciously.

"Who is Tong?" he asked.

"Tong is the Chinese guy who pays for Daniel's mom's house. I thought maybe they were together because they are around the same age but Daniel said no, it wasn't like that. He is really creepy. Real intense and serious, you know?" she shook her head.

"I'm still trying to take this all in," Lance said.

"Well, anything is possible but I think this may be a warning from the mafia," Ruth said, handing Lance a plate with a dripping cinnamon roll on it and a cup of coffee.

"The postmark was from a Sister Dolores at an orphanage in Laos," Lance said, filling in one blank and raising six questions at the same time. They continued to discuss the situation and sort through details and questions throughout the evening.

Ch. 18
Thurs. July 12, 2008
Daniel

I pulled the knife from my pocket and flicked it open. I cut the cable tie from her wrists, wincing as I saw the raw flesh.

"You've got to stop tearing yourself up. I need you to watch Charlie and its going to scare her to see you tied up," I said. She turned her brown eyes on me then and looked steadily at me. Sometimes her eyes were filled with fear, sometimes with pity. It was the pity that angered me the most. Grace was a girl with everything. Only 15, she had her whole life ahead of her. I on the other hand, had messed up more times than I could count. No one believed in me. Charlie was precious to me but since Shirley's death, I knew my life was over and I would either be on the run or in jail for the rest of my life. She nodded and I pulled the tape from her mouth. I turned to the cabinet and unloaded the groceries I found there. Mom had come through after all. I was surprised. She wasn't usually very reliable. There were cans of vegetables, soup, and a case of Grace's Diet Mountain Dew. I didn't know how she could drink that stuff. It made me burp.

"Can you make something for us to eat?" I asked. She nodded again. She hadn't spoken to me since we had unloaded Candace. I went to the front door and hammered 2x4 boards across it. Grace was stirring something in a pot. I went into the bathroom and boarded up the one window. I looked in the medicine cabinet and removed all the razors and pills. I found some ointment and carried it with me into the kitchen.

Charlie was sitting at the table with a pb&j, mandarin oranges, and a glass of milk. She was holding hands with Grace. They were praying. I waited an uncomfortable moment until they were finished. I sat down at the table and Grace handed me a bowl of soup. I handed her the ointment but I didn't say anything. She ate quietly and washed the dishes. She came into the living room, and after I boarded up the back door, I turned on the tv. She sat on the couch and pulled Charlie into her lap. Charlie had a stack of books she brought from the camp and she took them out of her backpack. One by one she lined them up along the floor. I found a football game on and I watched it just for something to do.

The silence was beginning to wear on me. Growing up our house was anything but quiet. There was always loud music playing and some man lying on the couch smelling of smoke. Sometimes it was cigarette smoke, sometimes not. I don't remember ever having my mom read me a book.

"Where is my Mommy?" Charlie asked for the thousandth time in 18 hours.
"Let's go to bed, sweetie," Grace answered saving me from repeating myself again.

I had been telling her the same thing for hours but she continued to ask every few minutes. The house was beginning to get dark and shadows were building in the corners and down the hall where they walked.

I watched them go, feeling exhausted and tired as I always did when the darkness built and my memories of Shirley's death returned. It was a moment of blind panic. She knew and she was so disappointed in me. She was going to tell everyone. It was the pity in her eyes that made me feel so small and weak. I had to show her I was still in charge. Gone was the respect and admiration I had gotten from everyone when they thought I was a success, a kid that had made it. I was supposed to be the one who changed for good. She seemed so surprised and dismayed. I had to wonder and would always wonder if she would have forgiven me like Candace insisted she would. Now I would never know. I couldn't think about that now. Shirley was gone for good and my life was over. I would not get to see Charlie grow up. I knew Grace would take good care of Charlie and get her back to Candace.

I thought back to the year I was 12. I had been going to Indian Oaks for two years and Mr. Richard had asked me to stay a few extra weeks to help him with construction of some new buildings. It was during the construction that I found the gold. I didn't know what to do with it. It was buried under an old shed Mr. Richard asked me to clean out. I was sitting on the ground with it spread around me when he came by. He explained to me that it was money that he had come into in an honest way that was supposed to be for good. He said that the mafia was looking for it so we had to keep it a secret. I didn't know what the mafia was. He explained that it was an organized crime group in Vietnam. I had heard of the

Vietnam War.   However, as I sat there looking at all those coins I had a vision of my mother sorting through garbage in a dumpster behind the public library looking for something for us to eat. There were needle marks on her skinny arms and it had been days since we had had a bath or brushed our teeth. As I sat there my heart began to harden and I began to curse God for taking everything from my mother and giving everything to this man before me who had to hide it and couldn't even use it.

My mother deserved better. When she wasn't drunk or high she was a good mother. She loved me and once bought me a guinea pig at a pet store. When our electricity was cut off we would wrap him in a blanket and listen to the little chirping sounds he made.

Once I got my hands on the gold, we are going to disappear and start over. A new life and a new start, just like I had preached for years to all the kids. Everyone could have a new beginning with Jesus. I wished I could believe that. All I had to do was wait for was Mom to come through with my plane ticket. She was thrilled when I contacted her a few months ago. She told me that she had gotten clean and had given up hope of ever seeing me again. She was going to be thrilled to meet Charlie. I needed some sleep. I might as well go on to bed.

I went through the house checking on everything and secured Grace's ankle to the bed with a pair of handcuffs.   She was lying on her side, her long hair covering her back and shoulders. Charlie had her thumb in her mouth and was closest to the wall. I knew Grace had put her there so she wouldn't fall out of the bed.

She had good instincts and would make a fine mother someday. I returned to the couch and lay down. It would be another long night but tomorrow when Mom showed up with my plane ticket, I would be in good shape. Finding Hope wouldn't take long.

Ch. 19
Fri. July 13, 2008
Waco, TX
Grace

I heard the chain rattle before my eyes were fully open, and I thought, "Another day alone with Daniel." My ankle was chained to the footboard of the bed. I checked on Charlie, who was sleeping peacefully and marveled at how well she had done without her mother. My Mom always said that children are resilient. I sat up in bed. The sun was streaming in the window. There was no curtain and I enjoyed the sensation of the warmth on my back. I began to pray.

Prayer was the only thing that had gotten me through this ordeal. I missed my parents terribly and I was heartsick over losing Shirley. Always in the back of my mind was what had happened to Shirley and what could happen to me if things went wrong.

"Dear God, please get me home." I felt tears filling my eyes and I took a deep breath, willing them away. I had to harden my heart or I would never make it. "Please keep Charlie safe and let me get her out of here. Please provide us with a way for escape. Please bless my parents." I had only spoken to my Dad once and I knew they were both frantic. Except for my Aunt Ruth and my grandparents in Memphis we were all each other had.

The air conditioner, a cheap rusty window unit came on blasting freezing air.
 I reached for the sheet to cover Charlie with. Awkwardly, I got to my knees and looked out the

window. I could see a bare back yard with a chain metal fence. In the distance was a convenience store. Good. If I could get away I could run to a phone. I checked my watch. 9:00 a.m. At camp I always got up at 6:00 to run. I hadn't been able to run since Thursday but I knew if I got the chance I might be able to outrun Daniel.

The door opened then and I sighed, knowing today would be like the other days with Daniel grilling me with questions about where my Mom had gone with his precious gold. "How am I supposed to know? I've been with you!" I told Daniel. He was such a jerk, I don't know how I could ever have been interested in him. He had fooled me like everyone else. I had admired him for his dedication to God and how he had been able to make it out of a bad childhood and take what he had learned and make something of himself. I knew he had been in jail and in a gang. He had told me all about that and some things from his childhood. In many ways I felt sorry for him. If he sensed this it only made him mad so I had to be careful of every word I said to him.

I was shocked to see a woman standing in the doorway. She was skinny and was wearing jeans. She had long graying blond hair and glasses.

"Hi, I'm Stacy, Daniel's Mom." she said in a voice that betrayed a lifelong smoking habit. I was so surprised I just stared at her. His Mom? I had met his mother at the camp and this was not the same lady. This must be his biological mother!

"She's still asleep, huh?" she asked walking close to the bed and looking down at Charlie. Finally, I found my voice, "Where's Daniel?" I asked.

"He's gone." She looked steadily at me then for a long moment. "Gone after your Mom to get the gold.

You know he found it, don't you? He found it under that old building." I had heard this story before. Quite frankly, I didn't care where the gold came from or who kept it, I just wanted to go home. I was sick of Daniel and the whole mess.

"Where did he go to look for her?" I asked, wondering what my chances for escape were now with only this skinny older woman watching me. I was sure her lungs were no match for mine, seasoned from years running track.

"I'm not tellin' you anything!" she shouted. "Daniel told me you were trouble, always praying for him and crying for your parents. My boy ain't never had nothin'. He ain't doin' nothin' wrong by going after that gold. He's returning it to the rightful owner. You don't know what we owe them."

I was quiet then, realizing she was emotionally unstable and I would have to tread lightly around her. Her shouting had woken up Charlie and she reached for me, eyeing Stacy warily.

"Gracie, I want my Mama." she whimpered against my chest.
"Oh, Charlie. It's ok. Remember, we are going back to pick up your Mom in just a few days. We are in Waco now. Mom is just fine and we are going to see her real soon." I repeated the story I had told her so often in the last few days.

"We are going back to get Mommy, soon? Real soon?" she asked.

"Yes, sweetie. Really soon." I replied looking pointedly at Stacy.

Stacy knelt by the bed and said, "Hi, Charlie. I am your Grandma Stacy. I am your Daddy's mom." Charlie looked questioningly at me and said nothing. Her blond hair was tousled and her blue eyes looked remarkably like Stacy's. I could definitely see a family resemblance between these two.

"Could we get some breakfast?" I asked Stacy. "Sure." she said with a smile. "I got Pop Tarts." Charlie scrambled over me and then stopped short. "Aren't you coming, Gracie?" she asked. I looked down at my ankle and waited.

"Oh, right. I've got the key here somewhere." Stacy began to search through her pockets. I watched her from the corner of my eye. She finally found the right key and unlocked the handcuff from the bed, leaving it dangling around my ankle. I suspected she planned to chain me to the table during the day. Daniel had trained her well.

We walked down the hall of the small musty house. Already I had memorized the layout. The windows in both bedrooms were nailed shut. There was a front door in the living room and a back door in the kitchen that I assumed led to a garage.

Stacy got us situated around the table and handcuffed my ankle to the table leg. She passed us the Pop Tart box and opened Charlie's package for her. She brought her a glass of orange juice and me a can of Diet Mountain Dew.

"Daniel says you like this stuff." she commented. "I do, thank you." I said.

"Do you want anything else?" she asked. "Could I have some ice?" I asked. She brought me a glass of ice and we ate our pop tarts quietly. Stacy tried to talk to Charlie but after a few attempts, gave up. Charlie would just look at her with big eyes and not say a word. After breakfast Charlie ran to get her backpack and brought out her few books and asked me to read to her. I did and Stacy, who seemed to be at a loss for what to do with herself, or us, wandered into the living room and turned on the tv.

"Honey, don't you want to come in here with me and watch cartoons?" she asked Charlie.

Charlie gave her a sober stare and said nothing. I asked Charlie to go to the bedroom and bring my bible. Stacy rolled her eyes when she saw Charlie carrying it to me.

My red bible was worn around the edges and looked like an old friend. I carried it everywhere. My parents had given me a Nook for Christmas and I had actually loaded 3 different versions of the bible on it but when it came to my daily devotions I just had to have my old red bible. Daniel had taken my Nook away as well as my phone and purse but he left me an empty backpack and my red bible. I read a couple of chapters and then Charlie asked for a bible story. I thought for a moment and then told her the story of Joseph, how his brothers sold him into slavery but years later he forgave them and helped them.

As I finished the story I noticed how quiet the house had become, and I realized Stacy had turned down the tv and was listening to us.

"You shouldn't be telling her all those fairy tales and crap about forgiveness," she stated, flatly. "Forgiveness is real," I said. "We can be forgiven of anything we have done through Jesus' blood. Including the blood that was shed when Shirley was killed."

"You bible thumpers are all the same. I heard all that stuff when I was in rehab. All you have to do is ask Jesus in your heart and your troubles will be over!" she said dramatically, swinging her arms wide and disrupting an ash tray on the side table.

"It's all a bunch of crap!" she said falling to her knees to collect the cigarette butts and ash from the already stained and dirty carpet. I decided not to say anything more, for the moment. I thought of my Mom and prayed again for strength and safety for her wherever she was and that Daniel would not find her.

The morning passed slowly. Charlie stayed close to me or wandered about the fenced in backyard. I encouraged her to get out and get some fresh air and exercise and I worried about her breathing the constant cigarette smoke. It was already making me nauseous.

Every few hours she would let me off the chain to use the bathroom and walk around. She always stayed close to me and seemed nervous that I would run. It actually did occur to me a few times to just push her down and run but I couldn't risk leaving Charlie behind. I had to have some way of getting her out safely.

The next few days fell into a boring pattern of repetition. Charlie and I spent our time together singing songs, coloring, and "doing school" as Charlie called it. She had a set of magnetic alphabet letters that we played with. I taught her the phonics song.

I knew Candace had been working with her to get her prepared for preschool. Little by little she warmed up to Stacy and allowed her to sit by her, stroke her hair, and read to her. It was very sweet to see them beginning to build a relationship. Stacy, for the most part stayed calm but I sensed a restlessness in her as the days went by. I wondered if I would wake up one day and she simply wouldn't be here.

I chafed to be home in my own bed with my parents and back with my friends at camp. I was bored. I had to pray for strength for each new day. I knew Stacy had been in touch with Daniel several times each day. As far as I could tell he had not found my Mom. I never did hear from Daniel or Stacy just where he had gone to look.

One night, after I had been there for over a week, Stacy suggested we play some board games. Charlie and I were only too happy for something to relieve the boredom. We played Uno and Chinese checkers with her. I could sense that Stacy was struggling with something. She seemed emotional and often appeared as if she was going to cry. Earlier in the week she would drink a beer or two at night and I was careful to watch Charlie and keep out of her way in case the alcohol affected her in a bad way.

After Charlie won at Uno for the third time and we were congratulating her and telling her what a smart little girl she was, Stacy burst into tears. She covered her face with her hands. Charlie looked at me with a startled expression. "I'm sorry I won, I am just a good jobber at playing Uno. Mama says I am. I'm sorry Grandma Stacy." Charlie said, patting Stacy's arm.

Stacy looked up at me and shook her head. "Everything in my life is so messed up. I was a horrible mother. I put my boy in bad places, now he is on the run. This precious little girl deserves so much more than I can ever give her. I can't keep her. I can't provide what she needs." She began to sob and laid her head on the table.

I knew this was my moment and I would have to work fast and be creative. I prayed for wisdom as I gathered up Charlie and said soothingly,

"Come on honey, let's get you to bed and I'll come on soon. I want to talk to Grandma Stacy." Luckily, she had not secured my chain to the table which indicated how distracted she was becoming. I walked Charlie down the hall and she slipped obediently under the covers. She was a great kid. I prayed with her, and left her door open a crack.

When I got back to the table, Stacy was dry eyed and smoking but the expression on her face was heartbreaking. The woman before me was a lost soul. I sat down at the table and took her hand.

"Sorry, I ruined the evening. I haven't heard from Daniel for a few days and I'm worried sick," Stacy said and began to cry again. I searched my mind for scriptures and prayed.
"Stacy, do you want to live in a new way? Would you love the freedom of being forgiven for everything you have ever done and know without a doubt that you had a Friend that would never leave you?" I had never led anyone to Christ on my own before and I had to find the right words. Stacy smiled and shook her head.

"Honey, I know you believe in all that stuff and maybe for you it's all ok but not in the world I live in," she said.

"Jesus lives in the world you live in. He wants to forgive you and He is just waiting for you to ask him for that forgiveness. I promise you that if you let me and Charlie go I will help you find your way. My parents can help you. Please take me home," I pleaded.

Ch. 20
Mon. July 16, 2008
Memphis, TN
Daniel

On Monday evening, a loud knock sounded at the door and Gary Stephens reluctantly climbed from his Laz y Boy and ambled to the door in his stocking feet. He grasped the doorknob painfully, his arthritic knuckles twisting with the movement of the knob.

"Just a moment, please." his voice was hoarse. "Who is it?" his wife Sarah called out from the kitchen.

"Dunno yet." He responded. Gary opened the door and looked up at a tall, white man in his twenties with blond hair. He was dressed casually in a red polo and khaki shorts.
"Can I help you, young fellow?"

"Yes, sir. My name is Daniel Johnson and I am a good friend of Grace's. I learned from her father, Phillip, that she and her mother Hope would be visiting here for a few days. I work with Grace and I've come to pick up some valuables that must be returned to the camp. Philip said I could meet them here. I hope I am not disturbing you. I know it's after 8:00," he said.

Gary scratched his gray beard and frowned. "I think you're confused, Son. Grace and Hope aren't here. In fact, I don't know anything about any plans to come stay for a few days, although we would love to have them both just as long as they would stay.

That girl is just as sweet as sugar. I call her "Shug". She's always been my sweetheart. Well, you might as well come in until we can get this hashed out. Come in, and meet Sarah, my wife."

Gary swung the door wide and motioned him in. When Gary turned away to call to Sarah, Daniel quickly closed the knife blade and put it in his pocket where he could get to it if he needed it. He pasted on a smile. "Good evening, ma'am. I'm afraid Grace and I have our signals crossed. I understood I was to meet her and Hope here. I spoke to her yesterday and she told me that they were planning on leaving this morning. Perhaps they've run into a traffic jam of some kind," Daniel said. They shook hands and Sarah motioned for Daniel to take a seat on the couch.

"I was just cleaning up the kitchen. Have you eaten dinner? I could fix you a plate. It wouldn't take a minute. You must be tired if you've driven from Texas." Sarah bustled into the kitchen, calling back over her shoulder, "Is sweet tea, ok?"

"Yes ma'am. I appreciate it." Daniel answered, feeling grateful for the Southern manners he learned from watching the older sponsors at camp.

"Have you tried to call Grace?" Gary asked. "No, I was just going by what she said, that she and Hope would meet me here." Daniel answered. "Well, it wouldn't do you any good anyhow. We don't have any cell reception out here in the country. Doesn't bother me a bit. I never went in for all that technology and stuff. Seems silly to send an email when you would do just as good to talk to someone in person. I know you kids use it, though." Gary said.

"Yes, sir." Daniel said.

"Gracie gave us quite a scare the other day. I guess you know all about that?" he asked.

"Yes, that's why I was so anxious to meet her today. I hope they are ok. Two women traveling alone and all." Daniel trailed off as Sarah set a plate and napkin down in front of him on the coffee table.

"This looks wonderful. Thank you so much." he said. Daniel looked down at his plate. His mouth watered. Meatloaf and green beans sat on a red plate with a mound of white potatoes swimming in brown gravy. He preferred brown and so apparently did Grace's family.

"So, do Grace and her folks travel much?" Daniel asked, keeping his tone light.

"Oh, I guess so, a fair amount. They used to have an RV." Gary replied.

"Did they ever camp a lot around here?" Daniel asked, inhaling his potatoes and gravy. He looked steadily at me then and I knew he was sizing me up.

"No, not around here much. They always stay with us. Seems like Hope always enjoyed Arkansas in the fall. It's real pretty over there. Phillip carried us on a trip there once."

Daniel finished his plate and wiped his mouth with a napkin. Sarah came in from the kitchen and he thanked her again.

"Well, I'm just thrilled to have Grace and Hope on their way. I can't think why they wouldn't call and let us know they were coming." Sarah said.

"Things have been real busy at the camp lately and the owner of the camp passed away just this week. They were probably just anxious to get away. I feel the same way. It was a real blow to lose her. She was a nice lady." Daniel feigned a yawn.

"Daniel, where are you going to stay in Memphis

while you're here?" Sarah asked. Daniel was taken by surprise. "Oh, um, I am not going to be able to stay. I'll have to head back. I'll just rest for a couple of hours at a truck stop or something. There is a big visitor center in Texarkana. I can sleep there and get some coffee and head on back to the camp."

Sarah and Gary exchanged a look that only a couple who had been married for 50 years could. Gary gave a small nod and Sarah said, "Well, if the girls are coming and you are going to meet them anyway you must stay the night here with us and let me fix you a decent breakfast in the morning. It would be my pleasure. I miss having someone to cook for."

Daniel looked uncertainly at Gary. "It's fine, Son. You don't want to be on the highway all night. Get a good night's rest and start fresh in the morning. What is it you are picking up from Gracie?" "Well, sir. I'm not exactly sure." Daniel fidgeted in his seat and scratched the back of his neck.

"She called me this morning, early, and said she had something for the kids for camp. She needed help getting it back to Texas and wondered if I could help. I told her I would be happy to." Daniel rose to his feet and thanked Gary and Sarah for their hospitality. Gary bid him goodnight and went about his nightly routine of locking up and letting the cat out.

"Well, now Daniel. Let's get you set up in the spare room. I'll put the girls in the front room. That's where Grace always sleeps." Daniel followed Sarah down the hall, pausing at a linen cabinet to unfold a beautiful puffed quilt that would easily fetch $300. They entered a room containing a large bed and a walnut roll-top desk. A picture window was covered in sheer curtains and in the driveway Daniel could see the outline of Tong Pham sitting in the truck.

He was very conscious of the barrel of the Ruger that Tong had shown him as he got out of the truck only an hour ago. Daniel had been amazed to find Tong in the seat next to him on the plane. He hadn't seen him in person in years. They had communicated mostly by email and cell phone for the last few years. However, he easily recognized the man who had visited him in juvenile hall when he was just 14 years old. He was thin with a long pony tail and sported a dragon tattoo on the top of one hand. Time had added a bit of weight to his face but the look in his eyes was more steely than ever.

Daniel had been in on a burglary charge and was scared stiff when a guard came to get him to see a visitor. He had been arrested before but never charged and he was terrified.

When he walked into the visitors' room, he made a deal with the devil that would change his life forever. Getting his Mom clean for the gold that Richard had hidden under the building. Tong had made it sound so easy. He asked if Daniel knew much about the Vietnam War. He told him how the gold had been stolen from his people and given away. Daniel had a responsibility to care for his mother. Tong told him it was his duty as a man since his father was gone. Since that moment he had lived in dread of what would happen before Tong and the Vietnamese Mafia were satisfied. What else could he have done?

Giving the gold to Tong meant getting his mother back. She was an alcoholic and a drug abuser.

Getting her the help she needed was a dream come true. How could he not help her? It meant that they would be able to live together again. Stacy had been "intercepted" as they called it, in the night, and taken to a house where she was kept under lock and key by specialty personnel hired by the Mafia. The weeks until her body was free from the grip of the drugs she had been poisoning herself with for years were horrific. Stacy wouldn't speak of those weeks but she was very grateful to have a second chance at life and was just as anxious as Tong to find the gold so they could finally be together as a real family.

Daniel sat down on the bed and put his head in his hands. He felt relieved to be alone. His stomach churned with dread at what he would have to do. Tong was not a patient man.   He now felt the responsibility for keeping Grace and Hope safe. He hadn't been able to save Shirley. He couldn't just sit there. He had to keep moving. He had to get information.

Daniel moved over to the desk and quietly opened the roll top. Inside, the pigeon holes were crammed with envelopes and he began searching. He was looking for anything that would lead him to where Hope was. He cast aside a calendar from Kaui and grabbed at a handful of postcards from Hot Springs, Arkansas.

On the back of one was Grace's handwriting.

Dear Granny and Papa,

We are having fun camping in Hot Springs. I got to touch the hot water at the park and Dad treated Mom and me to a hot spring pedicure at the Quapaw Bath House. See you soon.

Love,
Grace

Bingo! At least it was a lead. Daniel felt sick for a moment and knelt by the bed to clear his head in the only way he knew how. "Dear Father God, please help me. I know I have done wrong. I couldn't protect Shirley. I'm so sorry. Please help Hope and Grace. I don't know what to ask for, except wisdom to keep alive and keep moving. Please help me get the gold to Tong. Please bless my Mom and Charlie. Forgive me. Please forgive me..." He stood up. He felt some relief. God would find some way to provide for him. He would keep on having faith. He slipped silently through the house and out the door. Tong already had the motor running. They programmed the GPS for Hot Springs and began checking their iphones for campgrounds.

Ch. 21
Hope
Hot Springs, Arkansas

The next day, I met Rosa's supervisor Marla, and
she hired me on the spot. She was impressed with
my experience and enjoyed the meal I made her in
the kitchen as part of my interview. She didn't give
me a hard time about references or a resume. Rosa
had confided to me how desperate they were for
summer help.

"The Human Body Exhibit has had people
pouring in here like crazy. I don't understand it.
It gives me the creeps." she said, as we cleaned up
and prepared for the lunch rush.

"Do you mean the exhibit has actual cadavers?" I
asked, shocked.

"That's exactly what I mean." she said. We both
shivered at the same time. When I was here the other
day I was in such a fog about Grace's situation that I
had barely noticed. I assumed that the body parts
were wax figures or something. Gross!

I shook my head. I didn't have time to worry
about that. I had to find another place to stay.
I had moved out of the campground yesterday
afternoon, when the camp hosts came to my door
to leave a message that a young man had come by
asking for me. I spent a miserable night in my car. I
didn't sleep at all and alternately prayed, cried, and
called Phillip on the phone, to get updates and
comfort. I missed Phillip and Grace so badly.

I had to find someplace to get some sleep and
safety. I also missed my home and my kitchen.

Rosa put me to work on baking cookies for the boxed lunches they sold. This, fortunately, proved to be a calming activity and I inhaled the warm scent of chocolate as Rosa and I got to know each other. The difficult part was deciding how much to tell her about myself. I explained that Grace was traveling with some friends from camp before school started up again and Phillip was home working. She was divorced with one son in elementary school.

"I am doing some research for the camp and decided to take a job to supplement the camp's expenses. I'll go back home after school starts." I said. If Rosa wondered at my story she didn't comment. She struck me as someone I could trust, but I was not ready to confide in anyone. We made it through the morning's work and lunch rush. About 1:30, she said, "I usually take my lunch on one of the benches by the waterfall." she said. "Would you like to join me?" she asked, graciously.

"Oh... I didn't have time to pack a lunch this morning. I guess I'll just grab a Coke from the machine. I'll come sit with you though, it sounds good to get outside for a bit," I said. My stomach was growling. Rosa said nothing, just nodded her head and headed for the exit. I checked my pockets for change. I was almost out of cash. I was hesitant to use my credit cards, so I would have to find a bank to cash a check soon. I selected a Coke and pushed my way through the glass doors to the benches. Tourists milled around outside trying to keep their toddlers from falling into the beautiful churning waters that surrounded the outdoor area. There was a gorgeous, glass enclosed bridge on the second story high above our heads. The area was lush with green plants and flowers. It was almost like a jungle garden and smelled heavenly. I stood for a moment, enjoying the scenery and looking at the huge boulders around the waterfall.

I walked towards the bench and stopped short when I saw that Rosa had spread out two of the boxed lunches from the snack bar. "Let me treat you on your first day, ok?" she said with a kind smile lighting her brown eyes.

"Thank you," I said, tears welling in my eyes. I struggled for composure. Her sweet gesture was so unexpected.

"This is so thoughtful. I really needed a friend today," I said, my voice shaking.

She pretended not to notice and she handed me a wrapped sandwich.

"Try the roast beef, it's the best." The sandwiches were great, and we ate in a companionable silence. After we threw away our trash and settled back on the bench, Rosa dipped her head.

"I was taught to pray after my meal." I bowed my head to pray as well, relieved to find Rosa was a fellow Christian. I felt better at that moment than I had all day.

During the afternoon we worked to clean and prepare the snack bar and kitchen for the next morning. I swept and mopped the dining room and cleaned the bathrooms. Friday passed much in the same way.

On Saturday, I wandered over to the Ford Bathhouse determined to find a better place to sleep than the parking lot. I walked through the building and noticed for the first time the many dressing rooms located in the shower room. They were almost like closets, with a brown door. Just to see, I decided to hide in one.   I figured I could always pretend to be looking for someone if I got caught. It was about 4:30 when I went in. The bathhouse closed at 5:00.   I waited in utter silence until 7:30. It was quite possibly the most nerve wracking two hours of my life.

I could not hear anything and even if it meant getting arrested, I couldn't wait any longer. I was desperate to know if I had managed to pull it off. I cautiously opened the door that led into a hallway. It was dark. I couldn't believe it. No one had noticed me!

For the next two hours I crept through the halls of the building until I was sure that no one was there. Carefully, I rounded each corner, convinced that any minute someone would grab me or yell at me. My heart was beating furiously. Occasionally I stayed in one room or another, killing time and looking for a safe place to camp out. When I reached the lobby, I peeked out the window to the parking lot. I could hear the heavy footsteps of a security guard. It was dark and he carried a huge flashlight and baton on his belt. I wondered if that meant he didn't have a gun.

Crossing through the lobby, I entered the first of the heated pool rooms. The stained glass ceiling was huge and domed. In the moonlight, it was really quite peaceful. The room was extremely humid. I tried to breathe normally and found the heavy air very relaxing. I had a sudden urge to feel the heated water on my skin. I tiptoed to the edge of the pool and sat down. I slipped my flip flops off and laid them beside me. I dunked my feet into the water and watched the ripples. I wondered if there was some kind of silent alarm or motion detector that would go off if I jumped in. I slid into the water and gasped at the heat. I closed my eyes and sighed deeply. What on earth was I doing? I was miles away from home and my daughter had been kidnapped by a killer. I felt very much alone. I swam for a few minutes trying to take stock of the unique situation I found myself in. I missed my husband and longed to talk to him. I wanted to feel his arms around me, to hear his voice lead us in prayer as he had done last night. I was glad to be away from the campground. Daniel would never find me in this building tonight. I am at least safe tonight I told myself.

I crept up the pool stairs and sat dripping on the top step. After I had dried a bit I tiptoed over to a basket of towels and helped myself to one. I cleaned up the wet floor and wrapped up in the luxurious, fluffy towel. I checked out the lobby window again on the way back to the dressing room. I could see the security guard at a distance.

I spent the rest of the night sleeping off and on in one of the "resting rooms," used by the rich and famous in the old days. It didn't feel too restful, the dust was enough to keep me sneezing all night. I set the alarm on my watch for 4:30 a.m. I wasn't sure what time the staff would arrive. The bathhouse opened at 8:00 a.m. I also took advantage of the electricity to charge my cell even though I didn't dare use it. I feared it could be used to trace my location. I awoke stiffly and dressed in eerie silence. I hid again in the maze of dressing rooms. It would be a challenge to blend in with the morning crowd if the tourists were sparse. It turned out I needn't have worried. By 8:25 a.m. the foyer was flooded with women in their 60s, ready for their mud masks and sea kelp facials.

"I want to look ten years younger, Helen!" one lady with silver hair said. When her companion gave her a withering glance she turned red and mumbled, "Ok, maybe five."

I shyly pushed through the crowd and kept my head down. No one seemed to notice me going upstream to the exit. Outside the sunlight was bright and a steady stream of Town Cars were going past, husbands dropping off their wives at the spa for a day's worth of beauty and $1,000's worth of self confidence.

I looked across the street and noticed an Asian man with a ponytail, standing with his feet planted wide, wearing a pair of dark sunglasses. He seemed to be staring at me. He looked so out of place on Hot Springs' main street. There was a coffee shop next door and I ducked inside it, trying to convince myself that surely I had nothing to fear from a Chinese man with a ponytail. I ordered a coffee and looking over my shoulder I rushed into the ladies' room. I stayed there for several moments until my heartbeat returned to normal and I began to feel quite silly. I was becoming paranoid. Finally, disgusted with myself, I stepped out of the restroom into the crowded shop. My coffee was now lukewarm, but I drank it anyway as I left by the back exit. I rounded the corner to wait at the bus stop and was soon picked up by the Hot Springs transit.

I visited a church on the edge of town and took pleasure in the joy of worshipping with other believers. On Sunday evening, after hiding in the dressing room again and carefully checking on the security guard, I began to snoop around a little and found an unlocked back door. There is only one video camera that I can see and that is in the gift shop by the register. Luckily I saw the red light on it before I stepped in there. I took the opportunity to send a telex to Phillip letting him know I was safe but that Daniel was in town. He replied that Ken had not tracked down Daniel's mother's house in Waco. How frustrating!

On Monday, my work day was a good one. I was greeted warmly by Rosa and during our morning coffee break she shared some Mexican hot chocolate with me. She said she didn't like coffee. She said it didn't sit well with her stomach since she had had her gall bladder removed some years ago.

"So Rosa, tell me about yourself." I urged. Her eyes turned sad for a moment.
"Oh, there is nothing much to tell. I used to work at the Creation Museum in Ohio. I have a son. His name is Enrique. We live here about six years."

"Muy bien," I said. She gasped in surprise.
"Habla espanol?" she asked. "Well, I am not fluent but I was lucky enough to be part of a desegregation program in the 80s and I went to a Spanish-English school. I can speak, read, and write Spanish. I can translate some." I answered her in Spanish.

"You have a very good accent," she said. I looked at her and grinned.
"For a white girl?" I asked. She laughed. "I wasn't going to say that." I laughed easily with her.

"It's ok, that's what all my friends used to say. I grew up in Port Aransas and there is a big Hispanic population there and also in Corpus Christy." I said. She nodded and said pensively, "I have always wanted to go to Texas."

We went back to the snack bar to prepare for the noontime crowd. When we broke for our own lunch about 2 p.m., I asked Rosa to follow me to Walmart and have lunch with me.

"My treat. You have made me feel so welcome here." I said. I wanted to leave my car in the parking lot so that if Daniel discovered it he wouldn't know where I was staying or working. Rosa agreed and I explained that a friend was picking me up from work and we planned to do some shopping. She said nothing and ducked her head. I could tell she didn't believe me but she was too polite to say anything. After work, I caught the bus and headed back to the Bathhouse.

For the next couple of weeks my life was a quiet pattern of work and waiting. I continued to work in the Mid America Science Museum snack bar and hide in the dressing room of the Ford Bathhouse each night. Phillip checked in with me often by telex and I began to be concerned that someone would notice the telex tape becoming used but no one ever did. Phillip had proposed to me from Paris by telex while he was on a mission trip. As a twenty year old college student I had been blown away by such a romantic gesture.

Several nights I cried myself to sleep, the loneliness and grief over being without my child and husband almost overwhelmed me at times. Rosa was a great comfort to me. She seemed to sense that I couldn't confide in her. She didn't pry, just continued to hold my hand and pray with me at lunchtime. Without my Savior's love and Rosa's friendship I never would have made it through each day.

Ch. 22
Phillip

During the next two weeks, Ken continued to search for Stacy and Daniel and to research anything he could find on someone named Tong. There were several different leads he was working on, but since Candace didn't know his last name, his search was painstakingly slow.

One evening, when Ruth and Candace were hosting a sewing class at the camp, Phillip was sitting on the porch after filling Hope's hummingbird feeders. The house was quiet and he couldn't stand to be inside. Ken's patrol car came screeching into the driveway with the lights blaring.

"Get in!" he shouted.

Phillip stood up in shock and ran to the car door. "What is it? Is it them? Are they ok?" he asked, a frantic look on his face.

"We have located Stacy's house in Waco. It took this long but after we got the photo of the tattoo we took it to the bank who drafted the loan and a loan officer recognized the tattoo. Tong's last name is Pham." Ken said.

The drive took a couple of hours and the men made it without stopping. They neared the house at dusk and Ken reached into the glove compartment for his extra flashlight and ammo.

"Stay behind me at all times. Remember you are a private citizen, not a lunatic father. "

"I'll remember," Phillip said grimly.

Ken's knock at the door could have woken the dead six counties over. "Mountain Creek Police

Department. Open the door, please." His booming voice had no sooner ceased than his black boot was planted squarely in the door. With a powerful kick the door swung inward, revealing a dark empty living room. Again, he shouted, "Mountain Creek Police!"

Ken walked through the dark, heat filled rooms with Phillip right behind him. In one bedroom Phillip sank to his knees and picked up Grace's red bible. He knew it was hers. He had overheard her tell Hope one day when she thought they were alone,

"Mom, I hate it when I don't have my good bible on me, it's like not having your good bra on, nothing goes right!"

Hope had laughed along with her and he could still hear the sound of their laughter. Would he ever see them again?

"Look inside. Maybe she left us another message." Ken suggested.

Phillip rummaged through the bible looking for a note. There were several pages torn out. They were the book of Ruth. Grace had highlighted the verse:

"Entreat me not to leave thee, or to return from following after thee: for whither thou goest, I will go; and where thou lodgest, I will lodge: thy people shall be my people, and thy God my God."

As he read the passage he shook his head. "I'm sure she is trying to tell us something, but I'm not quite sure just what."

The men looked at each other with sudden understanding dawning on their faces. "She's going to Ruth's!" Ken handed the bible back to Phillip and reached for his radio, "Mountain Creek, be advised the house is secure and empty. Suspect is nowhere to be found. Need contact with

Port Aransas Police Department, repeat, Port Aransas, TX."

Ken looked at his watch. It was now 9:30 p.m. "We can be there by morning. Let me call Linda." He turned away and pulled out his cell phone. Phillip read again the verse from Ruth. When Ken came back Phillip said, "If I know my daughter she's converted Daniel's mother. Wouldn't that be crazy?"

"Yes, but I agree it would be just like Grace." The men left the house and got into the cruiser.

Phillip put through a call to Ruth to tell her and Candace of their plans. The women insisted on coming and could, under no circumstances be persuaded to stay behind. They jumped into Ruth's brand new silver Impala and after a quick stop at the camp to get Charlie's favorite toy, they began their journey to the coast.

Ch. 23
Hope
Hot Springs

About 7:30 p.m. Saturday evening, I was carrying some bags of French fries to the walk in freezer. It was dark in the storage area and I stopped suddenly, wondering as I crumpled to the cement floor just what I had managed to hit the back of my head on. I awoke at 9:30, squinting at my watch in the dim light, wondering why I felt such fear. Rosa was gone, I knew. Her son had a baseball game and I had volunteered to help Marla stock supplies. The museum closed at 8:00 p.m. and I doubted if Marla were still around. She had been in the gift shop ordering supplies with the gift shop manager.

I sat up feeling dizzy, a stinging lump at the base of my neck. What could I possibly have hit my head on? I struggled to stand. A shuffling noise made me realize I was not alone. My breath caught in my throat. "Who's there?" I said. A man cleared his throat. "Mrs. Stephens?"

It was Daniel. For a moment the light blinded me and I could see only his silhouette in the doorway. The freezer was to my right. I was too stunned to react. I heard screaming then my fists were clutching the neck of Daniel's shirt.

"Where is she? Where is she? What have you done to my daughter? Where is Grace?" I screamed, and pounded his chest with my fists.

"I didn't kill Shirley. I swear I didn't. Please come with me and I can explain everything in time. I had to do what I did. But I want you to know

I didn't kill Shirley." Daniel's voice was frantic.

"Where is Grace?" I continued to scream until I heard a deep voice snap, "Shut her up!" It was hard to see in the storeroom. The light coming from the snack bar dining room was bright and two tall figures stood before me. The hair on the back of my neck stood up and I stepped closer, desperate to make out a face. He turned sideways and I saw the long ponytail tied with a black band. It was the Asian man from the street I had seen a couple of weeks ago. He flipped on the light and I had to close my eyes for a moment. He held a gun in his hand and on his arm was a dragon tattoo.

"Shut her up, I said!" I flinched, his voice echoed harshly. He handed Daniel a roll of duct tape and he tore off a piece. He turned me around and taped my hands. I began to panic. I twisted and fought them both. I knew this was going to be my last chance to save my daughter. If Grace wasn't with Daniel then where could she be? I waited for the right moment, and amid their pushing, pulling on my arms, and cursing, I seized the opportunity and sank my teeth into the man's hand. I bit down until I tasted blood, then as he let go I pushed him with all my weight and ran.

With my hands tied awkwardly behind me and the tape flapping around my mouth, I slipped and slid over the stairs. Somehow I made it to the ground floor. I burst into the lobby yelling,

"Help! Help! Security! Security!" The man with the dragon tattoo was slowly making his way down the stairs. He smiled lazily at me. "Officer Smith has unexpectedly retired."

I closed my eyes. He was referring to our elderly security guard the day camp students affectionately called "Mr. Bill". Every day, he would stand at the door and greet each child and if they would shake his hand he would give them a piece of candy.

"You killed him?" I cried.

"He is, shall we say, just resting." he laughed, exposing yellow tar stained teeth. He grabbed my arm roughly and held my elbow in a vise like grip.

"I want what's mine and I want it now." he said, his voice low and his mouth close to my ear.

"Now, where did you hide it?" he whispered. I stared defiantly at him until he began to twist my arm painfully.

"Don't!" I cried.

"Tong! Stop!" Daniel was standing beside me, pulling me away. He put his hands on my shoulders to make me look at him. "Please, Mrs. Stephens. You have to tell Tong where the gold is. Grace is with my Mom. She's safe. You have to take us to the gold."

I turned away and started to protest but Daniel grabbed my chin with his hand. There was a desperation in his voice as well as his eyes.

"He'll kill you if you don't."

He looked over at Tong for a moment and then said softly,

"He'll kill me, too." I nodded my head and he pulled the tape from the side of my face.

"Ok, but we have to go back to Texas." I said and thought of my dear friend Rosa. I would never see her again or get to say goodbye to her.

"Where did you park?" Daniel asked Tong.

"East Entrance." was his curt reply. The Botanical Gardens were outside the East entrance. Keeping me between them, we slipped out the door and hurried through the garden when we heard a shout.

"Freeze! Hold it right there. You are trespassing unlawfully and I do have the authority to detain you." Daniel put his arm around my shoulder,

"Run! He's got a gun!"

I didn't know if he meant the security guard or Tong but I ran anyway. We crashed into the jungle plants as we climbed over rocks and slipped and slid over the waterfall. We were trying to get as far away as possible. I heard several shots ring out but I couldn't tell just which direction they were flying. Tong was crouched down behind a large boulder with a raft of pink elephant ears covering his face. I was looking his way when he fell over backwards and tumbled into the torrent of swirling water. It bubbled against his face and he looked up at me with an amazed expression.

"Where is it?" he whispered, as the current swept him past me.

Ch. 24
Hope and Daniel

"Daniel? Daniel?" I whispered, shivering. I couldn't hear a thing. A strong hand grabbed my shoulder and I muffled a scream when I saw Daniel's green eyes close to mine.

"Mrs. Stephens? Can you get up? I think Tong is dead." Daniel said calmly.

"What do you mean he's dead? Of course he's dead. People are shooting at us!" I hissed, fear rising in my heart like a living thing. My hands were shaking and I was breathing fast. Daniel took my hand.

"Come on, we've got to get out of here," he said.

"You've got that right. Where is my daughter?" I demanded.

"I'll take you to her. I can explain everything but not if I'm arrested. We've got to get the gold. You said its back in Texas?" he asked.

We had made it out of the garden and were hurrying through the parking lot to Tong's truck. It had begun to rain heavily. Daniel unlocked the door and let me in. I breathed a sigh of relief. Finally this whole nightmare would soon be over and I could hold my daughter in my arms. That would be...

"Watch out!" I screamed. The wet brakes squealed. A body lay in a soaking heap on the black pavement. Daniel looked at me in amazement. Slowly he got out of the truck and crept over to the body. It wasn't moving. He reached down and touched it. It must be the security guard. He picked up a radio and spoke into it. Daniel lifted a gun and a wallet. He came back to the car and gave me a somber look.

"He's dead. I called for EMS."

"Is it an elderly man?" I asked thinking of dear Mr. Bill.

"No, he is unconscious in the Human Body Exhibit. This guy is an ex cop according to his license. Must be extra security." Daniel said, starting the truck. He pulled out onto the road.

"Where is Grace?" I asked again.

"She's safe. I left her and Charlie with my Mom in Waco." he said.

"Oh." I let out my breath in a whoosh and prayed a silent, "Thank you, Lord."

I could see police lights and hear sirens behind us. I thought of Rosa with regret. What a dear friend she had become in only a few short weeks. I was so relieved to be going home. I couldn't wait to have this all behind us and see Grace and Phillip.

"Daniel? What happened? Why did you do all of this? What could have possessed you?" I asked, becoming angry.

"It's a long story and I will tell you everything from the beginning but the most important thing to me is that you know that I did not kill Shirley. Tong did."

"Who is Tong?" I asked, exasperated.

"This part goes back several years. You know I grew up hard. We all did, all of us kids at the camp."

"I know." I said, softly.

"My Mom was an addict. Drugs and alcohol. She did pretty good while I was a baby but the older I got the worse it was for her. When CPS stepped in and took me away from her, we were eating out of garbage cans behind restaurants to survive. I did ok in the first foster home I was in and I went to camp for the first time that year. That is when I found the gold. Richard had kind of taken me in and was showing me how to use tools, learn the carpentry trade. Kind of like Jesus, you know?" he laughed softly, shaking his head.

"Anyway, Richard had told me to clean out this old storage building. It was hot and I was tired so I flopped down on the grass beside the building in the shade. I lay down and I could see something sticking out from under the building. I pulled on it and it was one of those old wooden ammo boxes. I wanted to see it so I hauled it out from under the building. When Richard came looking for me I had it all spread out around me just looking at it. I had never seen anything like it. It didn't even look real. Richard told me to put it back, that someone from another country had donated the gold and it wasn't possible to exchange it for cash. He said he was going to leave it to the next generation of campers, that one day it would be possible to exchange but not right now. "

Daniel was silent for a few moments. I watched his face in the dark, the raindrops splashing on the windshield, making shadows across his features. He was a handsome young man I thought sadly. With a deep breath he continued,

"The next year I went to a new school, got in with a gang and got busted on a charge of burglary. While I was in juvie, Tong came to see me. I was scared to death. I was so afraid my new family would desert me. I knew at that point my mom couldn't take care of herself, let alone me. Tong didn't know I had found the gold. He just wanted me to look for it. I didn't tell him I knew where it was. I didn't tell him that for years. He said he could get my Mom clean, said there was a special clinic he could take her to, to dry her out, get her off the hard drugs, like heroin. We made a deal. He told me I was the man of my family and it was my responsibility to take care of her. He said I could pay off my debt with the gold. We shook on it and every few months he would contact me and remind me. My mom was taken in the night and dried out for two long months. Even today she won't talk about it. She is grateful, says we owe Tong her life. She told me I had to find the gold to make things right. I tried to tell her about Jesus but she doesn't understand. I don't think she will ever be saved." He shook his head sadly.

"Mrs. Stephens, I'm sorry I took Grace. I swear I didn't hurt her in any way. She is a wonderful girl and has a lot of faith. I can't say how sorry I am about Shirley's death. I never meant for anything like that to happen. I loved her." he began to cry.

In spite of myself I realized the truth in what he was saying. He didn't mean for this to happen. I placed my hand over his.

"I'm so sorry. I'm so sorry," he sobbed. I felt a lump in my throat.

"Pull over." I said hoarsely. I watched the mirrors carefully as he pulled to the shoulder of the road. He covered his face with his hands.

"How did it happen?" I asked.

"It was awful. I didn't know he had a knife. I called Tong at the beginning of summer to tell him I had the gold. He had to make arrangements to come and get it and have it converted to cash and then he wanted it in an offshore account. I don't know a whole lot about that kind of stuff. It all took several weeks. When you and Shirley found the gold that night I panicked. I just assumed that if I took Grace you would bring the gold right away. I never dreamed you would hide it." He gave me look then.

I smiled and said, "That was Phillip's idea. He said we had to have some assurance that you would not kill her and give her back. At that point, remember, we thought you had killed Shirley."

"Tong called after I got Grace tied up. He wanted the gold and he was furious when I told him what happened. That's when I had to involve Candace. I needed her to watch Grace while I went to Shirley's. I called her and said I wanted to talk to her about the gold without the police being involved. She said yes. Tong insisted on coming with me. I couldn't believe how fast it happened. He said maybe now I would take this seriously. It was a lesson to me, a punishment for losing the gold. We left her there alone and bleeding." he buried his head on his arms and cried. I cried too. I prayed silently for him.

"Come on," I said finally. "We have to get going. We still have hours to go. Do you want me to drive?" I asked. He shook his head no and pulled onto the freeway. Suddenly, I felt our roles had shifted. He was no longer in control. He needed me to take care of him. He was no longer the enemy. He was just what he had always been, a lost kid. Really what we all are without God.

For the next several hours we did not talk unless we had to. I felt that Daniel was too ashamed and spent to talk anymore. I was equally exhausted and excited for it all to be over. The storm continued. I kept thinking we would outrun it but we didn't. The heavy rain was a cleansing one. I felt it was somehow cleansing us of this whole nightmare of being apart. It was healing us, bringing us back together. We had suffered. Each in our loneliness. Now we are stronger and more appreciative of what we have.

The rain finally abated about dawn when we arrived in Port Aransas. "The jetty boat won't make its first trip until 8:00 a.m. Let's get some breakfast." I suggested a little coffee shop on the docks. Daniel brought back some coffees and egg sandwiches. I was reminded of the sandwich that Phillip made me when I left home several weeks ago. We stood by the car stretching and drinking our coffee. We still didn't talk.

"What are we going to do with it?" he asked finally.

"With the gold?" I asked. He nodded.

"What do you think we should do with it?"

"Do like Richard said and give it to the kids." Daniel said.

"I'm sure we can all agree on that. It really should be up to Lance." I said.

"He will never forgive me." Daniel shook his head sadly.

"It will be hard." I agreed.

As we watched the lights came on in Buck's and Willie the dog took up his post outside the door. I saved part of my sandwich and as I dropped it in front of him I thought about Sam, Grace's dog. I hadn't given her a thought in all these weeks. She would be glad to have her home. Daniel purchased our tickets and bought another shovel. We waited quietly with the early bird fishermen. It was almost over.

Ch. 25
Phillip

Philip and Ken stopped to fuel up and grab some dinner. Their own journey was uneventful. Ken kept in close contact with Hodge and the department. They reached the ocean side town about dawn and rolled down the windows to stay awake. Ruth's white clapboard house was in the older section of Port Aransas. The yard was immaculate with a flowering border of amaryllis and a small yard of closely cropped grass. Wind chimes hung from the top of the porch railing. There were no cars parked in the driveway. Ken pulled the extra key from the birdbath where Ruth told them it would be. He unlocked and opened the door. Phillip pushed past him shouting,

"Grace, Grace! Where are you? I'm here." He stopped short when he saw a tiny figure come down the hall.

"I know you. You're Grace's Daddy from the camp. You brought the piñata for the party we had before summer." Charlie stood in the living room wearing a pair of Scooby Doo pajamas, her long hair tousled.

"Where's Grace?" Phillip whispered, picking her up in his arms.

A harsh voice caught him by surprise.
"She's fine. She's just down the hall." A skinny woman with bad teeth held out her hand to shake. "I'm Stacy Johnson. Daniel's mother. You have raised a wonderful girl. She has shown me many new things. I'll go get her." She turned to go down the hall when Charlie said, "No, she's on the jet ski.

She said she had to go somewhere and rent a jet ski."
Charlie nodded confidently and put her thumb in her
mouth. The three adults looked blankly at each other
and then at Charlie.

"What?"

"Would you repeat that?"

"What did she say?"

Charlie nodded. "She goed to the beach place and
rented a jet ski. You know you can drive in the water
with it? I wanted to go swimming but she said I had
to stay here and wait for Mommy. Is my Mommy
with you?" She asked looking over Phillip's
shoulder.

Ken told her gently, "She'll be here soon. Can
you tell us anything else about where Grace went?
Did anyone go with her?" Charlie shook her head no.

"She borrowed Grandma Stacy's car." Ken and
Phillip looked at each other.

" She's got to be going to Carolina Key. How would
she know to go there?" Phillip said.

"She made a lot of phone calls last night, maybe
someone told her to come in the jet ski. I want to go
swimming! When can I go swimming, Grandma
Stacy?" Charlie wailed.

"When did she make these phone calls?" Stacy
asked.

"When you were at the store. Can I watch cartoons
now?"

Phillip put Charlie down and she ran to turn the tv
on.

"What is the make and model of the car?" Ken
asked.

"A 2000 Ford Uplander van. It's grey." Stacy
responded.

A knock sounded at the door and Ken muttered to

Phillip, "Backup."

Ken opened the door and let in two burly Port Aransas police officers. They motioned for Phillip to distract Charlie. He took Charlie by the hand out to the swing. As the door closed behind them, one of the officers produced a pair of handcuffs and said,

"Stacy Johnson, I have a warrant for your arrest for the kidnapping of Grace Marie Stephens, and Charlotte Ann Bradshaw."

Stacy obediently came to the officers and said to Ken, "Officer, please tell Grace thank you. I learned more from her in our few days together than I could have ever hoped. She saved my life, literally." Ken looked at her serene smile and shining eyes, and shook his head with disbelief.

"I'll tell her."

Within an hour a social worker had come to stay with Charlie until Ruth and Candace arrived. Ken and Phillip returned to the Port Aransas police department with the officers. The van was discovered in a public lot by the docks. The Coast Guard issued an APB for Grace and a jet ski. The ten minute ride to Carolina Key seemed like an eternity to Phillip, who sat in the bow praying and scanning the horizon for his daughter.

Ch. 26
Hope
Carolina Key

The sun was shining on the rippling ocean waves, so bright it made my eyes hurt. I stepped off the water taxi and walked down the dock. The huge granite boulders were pink and sparkling. The air was sultry, I inhaled deeply. There seemed to be a large crowd already here. I looked down the beach to the steeper area of sand dunes. Curious, Daniel and I walked over to the crowd. Several men in uniforms turned when we approached. Phillip was in the midst of them digging with a shovel. When he saw me I let out a yell and he dropped the shovel to swoop me up in his arms.

"Thank God!" he said. I grinned and kissed him. A scuffle erupted to my right. Daniel was running and several officers including Ken were grappling with him in the sand.

"Wait! He didn't kill Shirley!" I said.

"Daniel Johnson Ferguson, I am arresting you on charges of kidnapping, conspiracy to commit murder, and stolen property. You have the right to remain silent." Ken placed handcuffs on Daniel's hands and led him down the beach to the Coast Guard boat.

I buried my face in Phillip's shirt. "I missed you so much!"

"Where is Grace?" we both asked at once.

"Here I am!" I heard her sweet voice but I couldn't really believe it was her. She lay down a jet ski in the surf and drug it onto shore as Phillip and I ran to meet her. We grabbed her and fell down into the sand hugging each other in one messy pile. I was crying and trying to see her face.

"Are you ok?" I asked. Laughing and grinning she nodded.

"How did you know to come here?" Phillip asked. "Stacy was afraid to take me home, that she would get caught so I suggested coming to Aunt Ruth's. When we got here last night I called Mom but all I got was her voice mail. I called the house and only got the machine. Called Dad and it was out of range. When Aunt Ruth was gone too, I didn't know what to think. I called the camp and Lance told me that Mom had hidden the gold and I thought I would try here for a start. Lucky guess! So Dad, where's the gold?" she asked.

A Coast Guard officer came over then and said they had a ship to shore call for me. I boarded the large craft to take the call, wondering who it could be. It was Lance calling to make sure Grace had located us.

"Thank the Lord!" he said. "I am so happy for you."

"How are you doing, Lance?" I asked, thinking of him trying to go on without Shirley and what might be ahead for him.

"I am ok. I am throwing myself into the work of the camp. That's where she was the happiest. Incidentally, while I have you on the phone, I want to ask you if you would consider a different position at the camp. I had to fill the kitchen position. Bette is now the kitchen boss. Do you remember how Shirley wanted to fix up those cabins for a bed and breakfast?

Would you be willing to run that full time?" he asked.

I looked over my shoulder at my beautiful daughter, laughing, and scooping up golden coins with both hands and I knew what my answer would be.

"Sure, anything for the kids."

THE END

Epilogue

Phillip, Grace and I walked down the front porch steps of Aunt Ruth's house one last time. We had to hurry or we would be late. Ruth and Candace had been gone for hours, seeing to last minute details. The short drive was a pleasant one. We pulled up to the old estate house and went inside. We took our seats beside Lance who looked rather charming in a navy blue suit. Soon after Ruth gave a welcome speech she introduced Lance and he came forward.

"It is my pleasure to dedicate the Shirley Baker Home for Girls. It is my prayer that each mother and child who come here to live will learn to love God with all their hearts, souls, and minds. It is these qualities that will make a good parent." The applause was deafening and as I looked around the room I thought the gold could not have been put to better use. Anything for the kids.

Aunt Ruth's Famous Cinnamon Roll Recipe

Dough:
1c leftover mashed potatoes
2c water
1/2c warm water
3/4c sugar
3/4c butter
1t salt
2 envelopes yeast
2 eggs
8 1/2c flour

Filling:
1/2c butter
1c sugar
1 1/2t cinnamon

Icing:
3c powdered sugar
6T butter
1 t vanilla
5T milk
Add 2T fresh orange zest or 1/2c coffee to taste

Combine potatoes, 2 c hot water, butter, sugar, salt in large bowl. Mix well. In separate small bowl dissolve yeast in ½ c warm water. Let rest 5 minutes. Add eggs, 2 c flour, and yeast mixture to large bowl. Stir well. Continue adding flour until soft dough forms. Knead by hand on a floured surface until smooth and elastic. Place in a greased bowl, turn to coat. Cover with cup towel. Let rise inside your oven for 1 hour.

Ruth uses this time to crochet.

Punch down and divide in half. Roll one half into a rectangle and spread with ½ the butter. Sprinkle with half the sugar and cinnamon. Roll up tightly lengthwise and cut into 12 slices. Place in 13x9 pan. Repeat process with other half of dough. Cover. Let rise 30 minutes or until doubled. Bake in 350 F oven for 30 minutes. Combine icing ingredients and pour over rolls.

This recipe was originally given to Hope's mother Carol who passed it on to Ruth. Ruth added the orange zest and coffee to make it her own. She hopes you enjoy it!

Discussion Questions for Bible Study

1. List the strengths and weaknesses of each character.

   Hope:

   Phillip:

   Grace:

   Daniel:

2. What does Hope draw strength from?

3. Discuss Phillip's role as a protector of his family. How does he show courage?

4. What did Grace use to sustain her faith during her captivity?

5. What made Grace want to practice evangelism with Stacy?

6. Who does Daniel have to forgive?

   Discuss the difficulties in the process of forgiveness.

7. How does Daniel deal with his guilt over Shirley's death? How should he? List some verses on how we can overcome guilt and forgive ourselves for sins in our lives.

8. How does Lance show compassion for others?

9. How does Lance deal with his grief over Shirley's death?

10. What made Rosa show hospitality and grace to Hope? List verses.

Answer Key

1. Hope: strength, fear

   Phillip: courage, anger

   Grace: perseverance, evangelism

   Daniel: forgiveness, guilt, courage

2. Hope draws her strength from prayer and the love of her fellow Christians like Bette and Rosa.

3. Philippians 4:13

   I Corinthians 16:13

   Philippians 1:20

4. Grace maintained her courage by bible study and prayer.

5. Grace shared the gospel with Stacy to practice evangelism and show compassion for her fellow man.

6. Daniel must forgive his mother, Tong, and himself.

7. Hebrews 10:22

8. Lance shows compassion for others by using the money from the gold to start the girls' home.

9. Lance deals with his grief by asking Hope to start the Bed and Breakfast which was one of Shirley's dreams.

10. I John 1:7

   Ephesians 4:32